Flesh to flesh was what Rachel wanted.

Skin already hot, already damp. The feel of his lips against her thundering heart.

She locked her fists in his hair, pressing him closer. Even as the storm built to a crisis point inside her, she met, she ached, and she demanded.

Zack couldn't stop himself from taking. No matter that he had once imagined making slow, torturously slow, love to Rachel on some big soft bed. The desperation of what was overpowered any fantasy of what might have been.

She possessed him.

Obsessed him.

No mythical siren could have stolen his mind and soul more completely.

Dear Reader,

Welcome to Silhouette **Special Edition** . . . welcome to romance. Each month, Silhouette **Special Edition** publishes six novels with you in mind—stories of love and life, tales that you can identify with—as well as dream about.

April has some wonderful stories for you. Nora Roberts presents her contribution to THAT SPECIAL WOMAN!—our new promotion that salutes women, and the wonderful men that win them. *Falling for Rachel,* the third installment of THOSE WILD UKRAINIANS, is the tale of lady lawyer Rachel Stanislaski's romance with Zackary Muldoon. Yes, he's a trial, but boy is he worth it!

This month also brings *Hardworking Man,* by Gina Ferris. This is the tender story of Jared Walker and Cassie Browning—and continues the series FAMILY FOUND. And not to be missed is Curtiss Ann Matlock's wonderful third book in THE BREEN MEN series. Remember Matt and Jesse? Well, we now have Rory's story in *True Blue Hearts.*

Rounding out this month are books from other favorite authors: Andrea Edwards, Ada Steward and Jennifer Mikels. It's a month full of Springtime joy!

I hope you enjoy this book, and all of the stories to come! Have a wonderful April!

Sincerely,

Tara Gavin
Senior Editor

NORA ROBERTS

FALLING FOR RACHEL

Silhouette®

SPECIAL ▼ EDITION®

Published by Silhouette Books New York

America's Publisher of Contemporary Romance

Mary Kay, here's one just for you

SILHOUETTE BOOKS
300 East 42nd St., New York, N.Y. 10017

FALLING FOR RACHEL

Copyright © 1993 by Nora Roberts

ISBN: 0-373-09810-3

First Silhouette Books printing April 1993

Printed in the U.S.A.

NORA ROBERTS

is one of Silhouette Books' most popular and prolific authors as well as a *New York Times* bestseller. She has contributed to every Silhouette line and several short story collections. Demand for early titles has been so great they are being brought back as part of a special "Language of Love" collection.

Nora was the first author inducted into the Romance Writers of America's Hall of Fame and has received awards for her fiction, her creativity, her sales and her contribution to the genre. She has received lifetime achievement awards from the Romance Writers of America, Waldenbooks and *Romantic Times* magazine, bestselling title and series awards from B. Dalton, Waldenbooks and Bookrack, and numerous awards from booksellers, readers and peers for individual titles.

Nora Roberts is a consummate storyteller. Her generous spirit, humor, creativity, willingness to take chances and commitment to her characters, her writing and, most especially, her readers, have earned her fame worldwide.

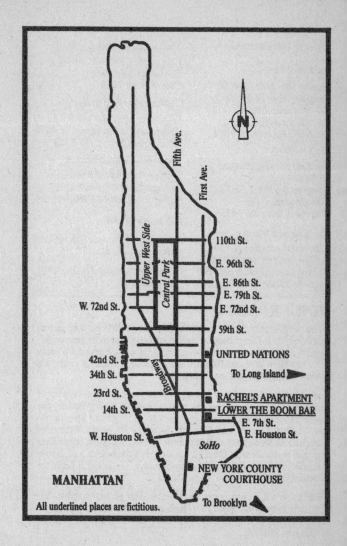

Fifth Ave.

First Ave.

110th St.

E. 96th St.

E. 86th St.

E. 79th St.

Upper West Side

Central Park

E. 72nd St.

W. 72nd St.

59th St.

UNITED NATIONS

To Long Island ▶

42nd St.

34th St.

Broadway

RACHEL'S APARTMENT

23rd St.

LOWER THE BOOM BAR

14th St.

E. 7th St.

E. Houston St.

W. Houston St.

SoHo

NEW YORK COUNTY
COURTHOUSE

MANHATTAN

All underlined places are fictitious.

To Brooklyn ▶

Prologue

Nick couldn't figure out how he'd been so damn stupid. Maybe it was more important to be part of the gang than he liked to admit. Maybe he was mad at the world in general and figured it was only right to get his licks in when he had the chance. And certainly he'd have lost face if he'd backed out when Reece and T.J. and Cash were so fired up.

But he'd never actually broken the law before.

Not quite true, he reminded himself as he pulled himself through the broken window and into the back of the electronics store. But they'd only been little laws. Setting up a three-card monte scam over on Madison for suckers and tourists, hawking hot watches or Gucci knockoffs up on Fifth, forging a couple of ID's so that he could buy a beer. He'd worked in a chop shop for a while, but it wasn't as if *he'd* stolen the cars. He'd just broken them down for parts. He'd gotten stung a few times for fighting with the Hombres, but that was a matter of honor and loyalty.

Breaking into a store and stealing calculators and portable stereos was a big leap. While it had seemed like a lark over a couple of beers, the reality of it was setting those brews to churning in his stomach.

The way Nick saw it, he was trapped, as he'd always been. There was no easy way out.

"Hey, man, this is better than swiping candy bars, right?" Reece's eyes, dark and surly, scanned the storeroom shelves. He was a short man with a rough complexion who'd spent several of his twenty years in Juvenile Hall. "We're gonna be rich."

T.J. giggled. It was his way of agreeing with anything Reece said. Cash, who habitually kept his own counsel, was already shoving boxes of video games in the black duffel he carried.

"Come on, Nick." Reece tossed him an armysurplus bag. "Load it up."

Sweat began to roll down Nick's back as he shoved radios and minirecorders into the sack. What the hell was he doing here? he asked himself. Ripping off some poor slob who was just trying to make a living? It wasn't like fleecing tourists or selling someone else's heat. This was stealing, for God's sake.

"Listen, Reece, I—" He broke off when Reece turned and shined the flashlight in Nick's eyes.

"Got a problem, bro?"

Trapped, Nick thought again. Copping out now wouldn't stop the others from taking what they'd come for. And it would only bring him humiliation.

"No. No, man, no problem." Anxious to get it all over with, he shoved more boxes in without bothering to look at them. "Let's not get too greedy, okay? I mean, we got to get the stuff out, then we got to fence it. We don't want to take more than we can handle."

His lips pulled back in a sneer, Reece slapped Nick on the back. "That's why I keep you around. Your practical mind. Don't worry about turning the stuff. I told you, I got a connection."

"Right." Nick licked his dry lips and reminded himself he was a Cobra. It was all he'd ever been, all he ever would be.

"Cash, T.J., take that first load out to the car." Reece flipped the keys. "Make sure you lock it. Wouldn't want any bad guys stealing anything, would we?"

T.J.'s giggles echoed off the ceiling as he wiggled out the window. "No, sir." He pushed his wraparound sunglasses back on his nose. "Thieves everywhere these days. Right, Cash?"

Cash merely grunted and wrestled his way out the window.

"That T.J.'s a real idiot." Reece hefted a boxed VCR. "Give me a hand with this, Nick."

"I thought you said we were just going for the small stuff."

"Changed my mind." Reece pushed the box into Nick's arms. "My old lady's been whining for one of these." Reece tossed back his hair before climbing through the window. "You know your problem, Nick? Too much conscience. What's it ever gotten you? Now, the Cobras, we're family. Only time you got to have a conscience is with your family.'' He held out his arms. When Nick put the VCR into them, Reece slipped off into the dark.

Family, Nick thought. Reece was right. The Cobras were his family. You could count on them. He'd had to count on them. Pushing all his doubts aside, Nick shouldered his bag. He had to think of himself, didn't he? His share of tonight's work would keep a roof over his head for another month or two. He could have paid for his room the straight way if he hadn't gotten laid off from the delivery-truck job.

Lousy economy, he decided. If he had to steal to make ends meet, he could blame the government. The idea made him snicker as he swung one leg out of the window. Reece was right, he thought. You had to look out for number one.

''Need a hand with that?''

The unfamiliar voice had Nick freezing halfway out the window. In the shadowy light he saw the glint of a gun, the flash of a badge. He gave one fleeting, panicky thought to shoving the bag at the silhouette and making a run for it. Shaking his head, the cop stepped closer. He was young, dark, with a weary kind of resignation in the eyes that warned Nick that he'd been this route before.

''Do yourself a favor,'' the cop suggested. ''Just chalk it up to bad luck.''

Resigned, Nick slipped out of the window, set the bag down, faced the wall and assumed the position. ''Is there any other kind?'' he muttered, and let his mind wander as he was read his rights.

Chapter One

With a briefcase in one hand and a half-eaten bagel in the other, Rachel raced up the courthouse steps. She hated to be late. Detested it. Knowing she'd drawn Judge Hatchet-Face Snyder for the morning hearing only made her more determined to be inside and at the defense table by 8:59. She had three minutes to spare, and would have had twice that if she hadn't stopped by the office first.

How could she have known that her boss would be lying in wait with another case file?

Two years of working as a public defender, she reminded herself as she hit the doors at a run. That was how she should have known.

She scanned the elevators, gauged the waiting crowd and opted for the stairs. Cursing her heels, she took them two at a time and swallowed the rest of the bagel. There was no use fantasizing about the coffee she craved to wash it down with.

She screeched to a halt at the courtroom doors and took a precious ten seconds to straighten her blue serge jacket and smooth down her tousled, chin-length black hair. A quick check showed her that her earrings were still in place. She looked at her watch and let out a deep breath.

Right on time, Stanislaski, she told herself as she moved sedately through the doors and into the courtroom. Her client, a twenty-three-year-old hooker with a heart of flint, was being escorted in as Rachel took her place. The solicitation charges would probably have earned her no more than a light fine and time served, but stealing the john's wallet had upped the ante.

As Rachel had explained to her bitter client, not all customers were too embarrassed to squawk when they lost two hundred in cash and a gold card.

"All rise!"

Hatchet-Face strode in, black robes flapping around all six-foot-three and two hundred and eighty pounds of him. He had skin the color of a good cappuccino and a face as round and unfriendly as the pumpkins Rachel remembered carving with her siblings every Halloween.

Judge Snyder tolerated no tardiness, no sass and no excuses in his courtroom. Rachel glanced over at the assistant district attorney who would be the opposing counsel. They exchanged looks of sympathy and got to work.

Rachel got the hooker off with ninety days. Her client was hardly brimming with gratitude as the bailiff led her away. She had better luck with an assault case.... After all, Your Honor, my client paid for a hot meal in good faith. When the pizza arrived cold, he pointed out the problem by offering some to the delivery boy. Unfortunately, his enthusiasm had him offering it a bit too heartily, and during the ensuing scuffle said pizza was inadvertently dumped on the delivery boy's head...."

"Very amusing, Counselor. Fifty dollars, time served."

Rachel wrangled her way through the morning session. A pickpocket, a drunk-and-disorderly, two more assaults and a petty larceny. They rounded things off at noon with a shoplifter, a two-time loser. It took all of Rachel's skill and determination to convince the judge to agree to a psychiatric evaluation and counseling.

"Not too shabby." The ADA was only a couple of years older than Rachel's twenty-six, but he considered himself an old hand. "I figure we broke even."

She smiled and shut her briefcase. "No way, Spelding. I edged you out with the shoplifter."

"Maybe." Spelding, who had been trying to wheedle his way into a date for weeks, walked out beside her. "Could be his psych will come back clean."

"Sure. The guy's seventy-two years old and steals disposable razors and greeting cards with flowers on them. Obviously he's perfectly rational."

"You PDs are such bleeding hearts." But he said it lightly, because he greatly admired Rachel's courtroom style. As well as her legs. "Tell you what, I'll buy you lunch, and you can try to convince me why society should turn the other cheek."

"Sorry." She shot him a quick smile and opted for the stairs again. "I've got a client waiting for me."

"In jail?"

She shrugged. "That's where I find them. Better luck next time, Spelding."

The precinct house was noisy and smelled strongly of stale coffee. Rachel entered with a little shiver. The weatherman had been a little off that day with his promise of Indian summer. A thick, nasty-looking cloud cover was moving in over Manhattan. Rachel was already regretting the fact that she'd grabbed neither coat nor umbrella on her dash out of her apartment that morning.

With any luck, she figured, she'd be back in her office within the hour, and out of the coming rain. She exchanged a few greetings with some of the cops she knew and picked up her visitor's badge at the desk.

"Nicholas LeBeck," she told the desk sergeant. "Attempted burglary."

"Yeah, yeah..." The sergeant flipped through his papers. "Your brother brought him in."

Rachel sighed. Having a brother who was a cop didn't always make life easier. "So I hear. Did he make his phone call?"

"Nope."

"Anyone come looking for him?"

"Nope."

"Great." Rachel shifted her briefcase. "I'd like him brought up."

"You got it. Looks like they've given you another loser, Ray. Take conference room A."

"Thanks." She turned, dodging a swarthy-looking man in handcuffs and the uniformed cop behind him. She managed to snag a cup of coffee, and took it with her into a small room that boasted one barred window, a single long table and four scarred chairs. Taking a seat, she flipped open her briefcase and dug out the paperwork on Nicholas LeBeck.

It seemed her client was nineteen and unemployed and rented a room on the Lower East Side. She let out a little sigh at his list of priors. Nothing cataclysmic, she mused, but certainly enough to show a bent for trouble. The attempted burglary had taken him up a step, and it left her little hope of having him treated as a minor. There had been several thousand dollars' worth of electronic goodies in his sack when Detective Alexi Stanislaski collared him.

She'd be hearing from Alex, no doubt, Rachel thought. There was nothing her brother liked better than to rub her nose in it.

When the door of the conference room opened, she continued to sip her coffee as she took stock of the man being led in by a bored-looking policeman.

Five-ten, she estimated. A hundred and forty. Needed some weight. Dark blond hair, shaggy and nearly shoulder-length. His lips were quirked in what looked like a permanent smirk. It might have been an attractive mouth otherwise. A tiny peridot stud that nearly matched his eyes gleamed in his earlobe. The eyes, too, would have been attractive if not for the bitter anger she read there.

"Thank you, Officer." At her slight nod, the cop uncuffed her client and left them alone. "Mr. Le-Beck, I'm Rachel Stanislaski, your lawyer."

"Yeah?" He dropped into a chair, then tipped it back. "Last PD I had was short and skinny and had a bald spot. Looks like I got lucky this time."

"On the contrary. You were apprehended crawling out of a broken window of a storeroom of a locked store, with an estimated six thousand dollars' worth of merchandise in your possession."

"The markup on that crap is incredible." It wasn't easy to keep the sneer in place after a miserable night in jail, but Nick had his pride. "Hey, you got a cigarette on you?"

"No. Mr. LeBeck, I'd like to get your hearing set as soon as possible so that we can arrange for bail. Unless, of course, you prefer to spend your nights in jail."

He shrugged his thin shoulders and tried to look unconcerned. "I'd just as soon not, sweetcakes. I'll leave that to you."

"Fine. And it's Stanislaski," she said mildly. "*Ms*. Stanislaski. I'm afraid I was only given your file this morning on my way to court, and had time for no more than a brief conversation with the DA assigned to your case. Because of your previous record, and the type of crime involved here, the state had decided to try you as an adult. The arrest was clean, so you won't get a break there."

"Hey, I don't expect breaks."

"People rarely get them." She folded her hands over his file. "Let's cut to the chase, Mr. LeBeck. You were caught, and unless you want to weave some fairy tale about seeing the broken window and going in to make a citizen's arrest . . ."

He had to grin. "Not bad."

"It stinks. You're guilty, and since the arresting officer didn't make any mistakes, and you have an unfortunate list of priors, you're going to pay. How much you pay is going to depend on you."

He continued to rock in his chair, but a fresh line of sweat was sneaking down his spine. A cell. This time they were going to lock him in a cell—not just for a few hours, but for months, maybe years.

"I hear the jails are overcrowded—costs the taxpayers a lot of money. I figure the DA would spring for a deal."

"It was mentioned." Not just bitterness, Rachel realized. Not just anger. She saw fear in his eyes now, as well. He was young and afraid, and she didn't know how much she would be able to help him. "About fifteen thousand in merchandise was taken out of the store, over and above what was in your possession. You weren't alone in that store, LeBeck. You know it, I know it, the cops know it. And so does the DA. You give them some names, a lead on where that merchandise might be sitting right now, and I can cut you a deal."

His chair banged against the floor. "The hell with that. I never said anybody was with me. Nobody can prove it, just like nobody can prove I took more than what I had in my hands when the cop took me."

Rachel leaned forward. It was a subtle move, but one that had Nick's eyes locking on hers. "I'm your lawyer, LeBeck, and the one thing you're not going to do is lie to me. You do, and I'll leave you twisting in the wind, just like your buddies did last night." Her voice was flat, passionless, but he heard the anger simmering beneath. He had to fight to keep from squirming in his chair. "You don't want to cut a deal," she continued, "that's your choice. So you'll serve three to five instead of the six months in and two years probation I can get you. Either way, I'll do my job. But don't sit there and insult me by saying you pulled this alone. You're penny-ante, LeBeck." It pleased her to see the anger back in his face. The fear had begun to soften her. "Con games and sticky fingers. This is the big leagues. What you tell me stays with me unless you want it different. But you play it straight with me, or I walk."

"You can't walk. You were assigned."

"And I can get reassigned. Then you'll go through this with somebody else." She began to pile papers back in her briefcase. "That would be your loss. Because I'm good. I'm real good."

"If you're so good, how come you're working for the PD's office."

"Let's just say I'm paying off a debt." She snapped her briefcase closed. "So what's it going to be?"

Indecision flickered over his face for just a moment, making him look young and vulnerable, before he shook his head. "I'm not going to turn in my friends. No deal."

She let out a short, impatient breath. "You were wearing a Cobra jacket when you were collared."

They'd taken that when they booked him—just as they'd taken his wallet, his belt, and the handful of change in his pocket. "So what?"

"They're going to go looking for your *friends,* those same friends who are standing back and letting you take the heat all alone. The DA can push this to burglary and hang a twenty-thousand-dollar theft over your head."

"No names," he said again. "No deal."

"Your loyalty's admirable, and misplaced. I'll do what I can to have the charges reduced and have bail set. I don't think it'll be less than fifty thousand. Can you scrape ten percent together?"

Not a chance in hell, he thought, but he shrugged. "I can call in some debts."

"All right, then, I'll get back to you." She rose, then slipped a card out of her pocket. "If you need me before the hearing, or if you change your mind about the deal, give me a call."

She rapped on the door, then swung through when it opened. An arm curled around her waist. She braced instinctively, then let out a little hiss of breath when she looked up and saw her brother grinning at her.

"Rachel, long time no see."

"Yeah, it must be a day and a half."

"Grumpy." His grin widened as he pulled her out of the corridor and into the squad room. "Good sign." His gaze skimmed over her shoulder and locked briefly on LeBeck. "So, they tied you up with that one. Tough break, sweetheart."

She gave him a sisterly elbow in the ribs. "Stop gloating and get me a decent cup of coffee." Resting a hip against the corner of his desk, she rapped her fingertips against her briefcase. Nearby a short, round man was holding a bandanna to his temple and moaning slightly as he gave a statement to another cop. Someone was talking in loud and rapid Spanish. A woman with a bruise on her cheek was weeping and rocking a fat toddler.

The squad room smelled of all of it—the despair, the anger, the boredom. Rachel had always thought that if your senses were very keen you could just barely scent the justice beneath it all. It was very much the same in her offices, a few blocks away.

For a moment, Rachel pictured her sister, Natasha, having breakfast with her family in her pretty kitchen in the big, lovely house in West Virginia. Or opening her colorful toy shop for the day. The image made her smile a bit, just as it did to imagine her brother Mikhail carving something passionate or fanciful out of wood in his sun-washed new studio, perhaps having a hasty cup of coffee with his gorgeous wife before she hurried off to her midtown office.

And here she was, waiting for a cup of what would certainly be very bad coffee in a downtown precinct house filled with the sight and smells and sounds of misery.

Alex handed her the coffee, then eased down on the desk beside her.

"Thanks." She sipped, winced, and watched a couple of hookers strut out of the holding cells. A tall, bleary-eyed man with a night's worth of stubble shifted around them and followed a uniform through the door that led down to the cells. Rachel gave a little sigh.

"What's wrong with us, Alexi?"

He grinned again and slipped an arm around her. "What? Just because we like slogging through the dregs for a living, for little pay and less gratitude? Nothing. Not a thing."

She chuckled and fueled her system with the motor oil disguised as coffee. "At least you just got a promotion. Detective Stanislaski."

"Can't help it if I'm good. You, on the other hand, are spinning your wheels putting criminals back on the streets I'm risking life and limb to keep clean."

She snorted, scowling at him over the brim of the paper cup. "Most of the people I represent aren't doing anything more than trying to survive."

"Sure—by stealing, cheating, and assaulting."

Her temper began to heat. "I went to court this morning to represent an old man who'd copped some disposable razors. A real desperate case, that one. I guess they should have locked him up and thrown away the key."

"So it's okay to steal as long as what you take isn't particularly valuable?"

"He needed help, not a jail sentence."

"Like that creep you got off last month who terrorized two old shopkeepers, wrecked their store and stole the pitiful six hundred in the till?"

She'd hated that one, truly hated it. But the law was clear, and had been made for a reason. "Look, you guys blew that one. The arresting officer didn't read him his rights in his native language or arrange for a translator. My client barely understood a dozen words of English." She shook her head before Alex could jump into one of his more passionate arguments. "I don't have time to debate the law with you. I need to ask you about Nicholas LeBeck."

"What about him? You got the report."

"You were the arresting officer."

"Yeah—so? I was on my way home, and I happened to see the broken window and the light inside. When I went to investigate, I saw the perpetrator coming through the window carrying a sackful of electronics. I read him his rights and brought him in."

"What about the others?"

Alex shrugged and finished off the last couple of swallows of Rachel's coffee. "Nobody around but LeBeck."

"Come on, Alex, twice as much was taken from the store as what my client allegedly had in his bag."

"I figure he had help, but I didn't see anyone else. And your client exercised his right to remain silent. He has a healthy list of priors."

"Kid stuff."

Alex sneered. "You could say he didn't spend his childhood in the Boy Scouts."

"He's a Cobra."

"He had the jacket," Alex agreed. "And the attitude."

"He's a scared kid."

With a sound of disgust, Alex chucked the empty cup into a wastebasket. "He's no kid, Rach."

"I don't care how old he is, Alex. Right now he's a scared kid sitting in a cell and trying to pretend he's tough. It could have been you, or Mikhail—even Tash or me—if it hadn't been for Mama and Papa."

"Hell, Rachel."

"It could have been," she insisted. "Without the family, without all the hard work and sacrifices, any one of us could have gotten sucked into the streets. You know it."

He did. Why did she think he'd become a cop? "The point is, we didn't. It's a basic matter of what's right and what's wrong."

"Sometimes people make bad choices because there's no one around to help them make good ones."

They could have spent hours debating the many shades of justice, but he had to get to work. "You're too softhearted, Rachel. Just make sure it doesn't lead to being softheaded. The Cobras are one of the roughest gangs going. Don't start thinking your client's a candidate for Boys' Town."

Rachel straightened, pleased that her brother remained slouched against the desk. It meant they were eye to eye. "Was he carrying a weapon?"

Alex sighed. "No."

"Did he resist arrest?"

"No. But that doesn't change what he was doing, or what he is."

"It might not change what he was doing—allegedly—but it might very well say something about what he is. Preliminary hearing's at two."

"I know."

She smiled again and kissed him. "See you there."

"Hey, Rachel." She turned at the doorway and looked back. "Want to catch a movie tonight?"

"Sure." She'd made it to the outside in two steps when her name was called again, more formally this time.

"Ms. Stanislaski!"

She paused, flipping her hair back with one hand as she looked over her shoulder. It was the tired-eyed, stubble-faced man she'd noticed before. Hard to miss, she reflected as he hurried toward her. He was over six feet by an inch or so, and his baggy sweatshirt was held up by a pair of broad shoulders. Faded jeans, frayed at the cuffs, white at the stress points, fit well over long legs and narrow hips.

It would have been hard not to miss the anger, too. It radiated from him, and it was reflected in steel-blue eyes set deep in a rough, hollow-cheeked face.

"Rachel Stanislaski?"

"Yes."

He caught her hand and, in the process of shaking it, dragged her down a couple of steps. He might look lean and mean, Rachel thought, but he had the grip of a bear trap.

"I'm Zackary Muldoon," he said, as if that explained everything.

Rachel only lifted a brow. He certainly looked fit to spit nails, and after that brief taste of his strength she wouldn't have put the feat past him. But she wasn't easily intimidated, particularly when she was standing in an area swarming with cops.

"Can I help you, Mr. Muldoon?"

"I'm counting on it." He dragged a big hand through a tousled mop of hair as dark as her own. He swore and took her elbow to pull her down the rest of the steps. "What's it going to take to get him out? And why the hell did he call you and not me? And why in God's name did you let him sit in a cell all night? What kind of lawyer are you?"

Rachel shook her arm free—no easy task—and prepared to use her briefcase as a weapon if it became necessary. She'd heard about the black Irish and their tempers. But Ukrainians were no slouches, either.

"Mr. Muldoon, I don't know who you are or what you're talking about. And I happen to be very busy." She'd managed two steps when he whirled her around. Rachel's tawny eyes narrowed dangerously. "Look, Buster—"

"I don't care how busy you are, I want some answers. If you don't have time to help Nick, then we'll get another lawyer. God knows why he chose some fancy broad in a designer suit in the first place." His blue eyes shot fire, the Irish poet's mouth hardening into a sneer.

She sputtered, angry color flagging both cheeks. She jabbed one stiffened, clear-tipped finger in his chest. "*Broad?* You just watch who you call *broad,* pal, or—"

"Or you'll get your boyfriend to lock me in a cell?" Zack suggested. Yeah, that was definitely a fancy face, he thought in disgust. Butter-soft skin in pale gold, and eyes like good Irish whiskey. What he needed was a street fighter, and he'd gotten society. "I don't know what kind of defense Nick expects from some woman who spends her time kissing cops and making dates when she's supposed to be working."

"It's none of your business what I—" She took a deep breath. Nick. "Are you talking about Nicholas LeBeck?"

"Of course I'm talking about Nicholas LeBeck. Who the hell do you think I'm talking about?" His black brows drew together over his furious eyes. "And you'd better come up with some answers, lady, or you're going to be off his case and out on your pretty butt."

"Hey, Rachel!" An undercover cop dressed like a wino sidled up behind her. He eyed Zack. "Any problem here?"

"No." Though her eyes were blazing, she offered him a half smile. "No, I'm fine, Matt. Thanks." She edged over to one side and lowered her voice. "I don't owe you any answers, Muldoon. And insulting me is a poor way to gain my cooperation."

"You're paid to cooperate," he told her. "Just how much are you hosing the boy for?"

"Excuse me?"

"What's your fee, sugar?"

Her teeth set. The way she saw it, *sugar* was only a marginal step up from *broad*. "I'm a public defender, Muldoon, assigned to LeBeck's case. That means he doesn't owe me a damn thing. Just like I don't owe you."

"A PD?" He all but backed her off the sidewalk and into the building. "What the devil does Nick need a PD for?"

"Because he's broke and unemployed. Now, if you'll excuse me . . ." She set a hand on his chest and shoved. She'd have been better off trying to shove away the brick building at her back.

"He lost his job? But . . ." The words trailed off. This time Rachel read something other than anger in his eyes. Weariness, she thought. A trace of despair. Resignation. "He could have come to me."

"And who the hell are you?"

Zack rubbed a hand over his face. "I'm his brother."

Rachel pursed her lips, lifted a brow. She knew how the gangs worked, and though Zack looked rough-and-ready enough to fit in with the Cobras, he also looked too old to be a card-carrying member.

"Don't the Cobras have an age limit?"

"What?" He let his hand drop and focused on her again with a fresh oath. "Do I look like I belong to a street gang?"

With her head tilted, Rachel ran her gaze from his battered high-tops to his shaggy dark head. He had the look of a street tough, certainly of a man who could bulldoze his way down alleys, pounding rivals with those big-fisted hands. The hard, hollowed face and hot eyes made her think he'd enjoy cracking skulls, particularly hers. "Actually, you could pass. And your manners certainly reflect the code. Rude, abrasive, and rough."

He didn't give a damn what she thought of his appearance, or his manners, but it was time they set the record straight. "I'm Nick's brother—stepbrother, if you want to be technical. His mother married my father. Get it?"

Her eyes remained wary, but there was some interest there now. "He said he didn't have any relatives."

For an instant, she thought she saw hurt in those steel-blue depths. Then it was gone, hardened away. "He's got me, whether he likes it or not. And I can afford a real lawyer, so why don't you fill me in, and I'll take it from there."

This time she didn't merely set her teeth, she practically snarled. "I happen to be a *real* lawyer, Muldoon. And if LeBeck wants other counsel, he can damn well ask for it himself.''

He struggled to find the patience that always seemed to elude him. ''We'll get into that later. For now, I want to know what the hell's going on.''

''Fine.'' She snapped the word out as she looked at her watch. ''You can have fifteen minutes of my time, providing you take it while I eat. I have to be back in court in an hour.''

Chapter Two

From the way she looked—elegant sex in a three-piece suit—Zack figured her for one of the trendy little restaurants that served complicated pasta dishes and white wine. Instead, she stalked down the street, her long legs eating up the sidewalk so that he didn't have to shorten his pace to keep abreast.

She stopped at a vendor and ordered a hot dog—loaded—with a soft drink, then stepped aside to give Zack room to make his selection. The idea of eating anything that looked like a hot dog at what he considered the crack of dawn had his stomach shriveling. Zack settled for a soft drink—the kind loaded with sugar and caffeine—and a cigarette.

Rachel took the first bite, licked mustard off her thumb. Over the scent of onions and relish, Zack caught a trace of her perfume. It was like walking through the jungle, he thought with a frown. All those ripe, sweaty smells, and then suddenly, unexpectedly, you could come across some exotic, seductive vine tangled with vivid flowers.

"He's charged with burglary," Rachel said with her mouth full. "Not much chance of shaking it. He was apprehended climbing out of the window with several thousand dollars' worth of stolen merchandise in his possession."

"Stupid." Zack downed half the soft drink in a swallow. "He doesn't have to steal."

"That's neither here nor there. He was caught, he was charged, and he doesn't deny the act. The DA's willing to deal, offer probation and community service, if Nick cooperates."

Zack chuffed out smoke. "Then he'll cooperate."

Rachel's left brow lifted, then settled. She had no doubt Zackary Muldoon thought he could prod, push or punch anybody into anything. "I sincerely doubt it. He's scared, but he's stubborn. And he's loyal to the Cobras."

Zack said something foul about the Cobras. Rachel was forced to agree. "Well, that may be, but it doesn't change the bottom line. His record is fairly lengthy, and it won't be easy to get around it. It's also mostly hustle and jive. The fact that this is his first step into the big leagues might help reduce his sentence. I think I can get him off with three years. If he behaves, he'll only serve one."

Zack's fingers dug into the aluminum can, crushing it. Fear settled sickly in his stomach. "I don't want him to go to prison."

"Muldoon, I'm a lawyer, not a magician."

"They got back the stuff he took, didn't they?"

"That doesn't negate the crime, but yes. Of course, there's several thousand more outstanding."

"I'll make it good." Somehow. Zack heaved the can toward a waste can. It tipped the edge, joggled, then fell inside. "Listen, I'll make restitution on what was stolen. Nick's only nineteen. If you can get the DA to try him as a minor, it would go easier."

"The state's tough on gang members, and with his record I don't think it would happen."

"If you can't do it, I'll find someone who can." Zack threw up a hand before she could tear into him. "I know I came down on you before. Sorry. I work nights, and I'm not my best in the morning." Even that much of an apology grated on him, but he needed her. "I get a call an hour ago from one of Nick's friends telling me he's been in jail all night. When I get down here and see him, it's the same old story. I don't need you. I don't need anybody. I'm handling it." He tossed down his cigarette, crushed it out, lit another. "And I know he's scared down to the bone." With something close to a sigh, he jammed his hands in his pockets. "I'm all he's got, Ms. Stanislaski. Whatever it takes, I'm not going to see him go to prison."

It was never easy for her to harden her heart, but she tried. She wiped her hands carefully on a paper napkin. "Have you got enough money to cover the losses? Fifteen thousand?"

He winced, but nodded. "I can get it."

"It'll help. How much influence do you have over Nick?"

"Next to none." He smiled, and Rachel was surprised to note that the smile held considerable charm.

"But that can change. I've got an established business, and a two-bedroom apartment. I can get you professional and character references, whatever you need. My record's clean— Well, I did spend thirty days in the brig when I was in the navy. Bar fight." He shrugged it off. "I don't guess they'd hold it against me, since it was twelve years ago."

Rachel turned the possibilities over in her mind. "If I'm reading you right, you want me to try to get the court to turn Nick over to your care."

"The probation and community service. A responsible adult to look out for him. All the damages paid."

"You might not be doing him any favor, Muldoon."

"He's my brother."

That she understood perfectly. Rachel cast her eyes skyward as the first drop of rain fell. "I've got to get back to the office. If you've got the time, you can walk with me. I'll make some calls, see what I can do."

A bar, Rachel thought with a sigh as she tried to put together a rational proposition for the hearing that afternoon. Why did the man have to own a bar? She supposed it suited him—the big shoulders, the big hands, the crooked nose that she assumed had been broken. And, of course, the rough, dark Irish looks that matched his temper.

But it would have been so much nicer if she could tell the judge that Zackary Muldoon owned a nice men's shop in midtown. Instead, she was going to ask a judge to hand over the responsibility and the guardianship of a nineteen-year-old boy—with a record and an attitude—to his thirty-two-year-old stepbrother, who ran an East Side bar called Lower the Boom.

There was a chance, a slim one. The DA was still pushing for names, but the shop owner had been greatly mollified with the promise of settlement. No doubt he'd inflated the price of his merchandise, but that was Muldoon's problem, not hers.

She didn't have much time to persuade the DA that he didn't want to try Nick as an adult. Taking what information she'd managed to pry out of Zack, she snagged opposing counsel and settled into one of the tiny conference rooms in the courthouse.

"Come on, Haridan, let's clean this mess up and save the court's time and the taxpayers' money. Putting this kid in jail isn't the answer."

Haridan, balding on top and thick through the middle, eased his bulk into a chair. "It's my answer, Stanislaski. He's a punk. A gang member with a history of antisocial behavior."

"Some tourist scams and some pushy-shovey."

"Assault."

"Charges were dropped. Come on, we both know it's minor-league. *He's* minor-league. We've got a scared, troubled kid looking for his place with a gang. We want him out of the gang, no question. But jail isn't the way." She held up a hand before Haridan could interrupt. "Look, his stepbrother is willing to help—not only by paying for property you have absolutely no proof my client stole, but by taking responsibility. Giving LeBeck a job, a home, supervision. All you have to do is agree to handling LeBeck as a minor."

"I want names."

"He won't give them." Hadn't she gone back down and harassed Nick for nearly an hour to try to pry one loose? "You can put him away for ten years, and you still won't get one. So what's the point? You haven't got a hardened criminal here—yet. Let's not make him one."

They knocked that back and forth, and Haridan softened. Not out of the goodness of his heart, but because his plate was every bit as full as Rachel's. He had neither the time nor the energy to pursue one punk kid through the system.

"I'm not dropping it down from burglary to night-time breaking and entering." On that he was going to stand firm, but he would throw her a crumb. "Even if we agree to handle him as a juvie, the judge isn't going to let him walk with probation."

Rachel gathered up her briefcase. "Just leave the judge to me. Who'd we pull?"

Haridan grinned. "Beckett."

Marlene C. Beckett was an eccentric. Like a magician, she pulled unusual sentences out of her judge's robes as if they were little white rabbits. She was in her midforties, dashingly attractive, with a single streak of white hair that swept through a wavy cap of fire-engine red.

Personally, Rachel liked her a great deal. Judge Beckett was a staunch feminist and former flower child who had proven that a woman—an unmarried, career-oriented woman—could be successful and intelligent without being abrasive or whiny. She might have been in a man's world, but Judge Beckett was all woman. Rachel respected her, admired her, even hoped to follow in her footsteps one day.

She just wished she'd been assigned to another judge.

As Beckett listened to her unusual plea, Rachel felt her stomach sinking down to her knees. Beckett's lips were pursed. A bad sign. One perfectly manicured nail was tapping beside the gavel. Rachel caught the judge studying the defendant, and Zack, who sat in the front row behind him.

"Counselor, you're saying the defendant will make restitution for all properties lost, and that though the state is agreeable that he be tried as a minor, you don't want him bound over for trial."

"I'm proposing that trial may be waived, Your Honor, given the circumstances. Both the defendant's mother and stepfather are deceased. His mother died five years ago, when the defendant was fourteen, and his stepfather died last year. Mr. Muldoon is willing and able to take responsibility for his stepbrother. If it please the court, the defense suggests that once restitution is made, and a stable home arranged, a trial would be merely an unproductive way of punishing my client for a mistake he already deeply regrets."

With what might have been a snort, Beckett cast a look at Nick. "Do you deeply regret bungling your attempt at burglary, young man?"

Nick lifted one shoulder and looked surly. A sharp rap on the back of the head from his stepbrother had him snarling. "Sure, I—" He glanced at Rachel. The warning in her eyes did more to make him subside than the smack. "It was stupid."

"Undoubtedly," Judge Beckett agreed. "Mr. Haridan, what is your stand on this?"

"The district attorney's office is not willing to drop charges, Your Honor, though we will agree to regard the defendant as a juvenile. An offer to lessen or drop charges was made—if the defendant would provide the names of his accomplices."

"You want him to squeal on those he—mistakenly, I'm sure—considers friends?" Beckett lifted a brow at Nick. "No dice?"

"No, ma'am."

She made some sound that Rachel couldn't interpret, then pointed at Zack. "Stand up... Mr. Muldoon, is it?"

Ill at ease, Zack did so. "Ma'am? Your Honor?"

"Where were you when your young brother was getting himself mixed up with the Cobras?"

"At sea. I was in the navy until two years ago, when I came back to take over my father's business."

"What rank?"

"Chief petty officer, ma'am."

"Mm-hmm..." She took his measure, as a judge and as a woman. "I've been in your bar—a few years back. You used to serve an excellent manhattan."

Zack grinned. "We still do."

"Are you of the opinion, Mr. Muldoon, that you can keep your brother out of trouble and make a responsible citizen of him?"

"I... I don't know, but I want a chance to try."

Beckett tapped her fingers and sat back. "Have a seat. Ms. Stanislaski, the court is not of the opinion that a trial would be out of place in this matter—"

"Your Honor—"

Beckett cut Rachel off with a single gesture. "I haven't finished. I'm going to set bail at five thousand dollars."

This brought on an objection from the DA that was dealt with in exactly the same manner.

"I'm also going to grant the defendant what we'll call a provisionary probation. Two months," Beckett said, folding her hands. "I will set the trial date for two months from today. If during that two-month period the defendant is found to be walking the straight and narrow, is gainfully employed, refrains from associating with known members of the Cobras and has not committed any crime, this court will be amenable to extending that probation, with the likelihood of a suspended sentence."

"Your Honor," Haridan puffed out, "how can we be certain the defendant won't waltz in here in two months and claim to have upheld the provisions?"

"Because he will be supervised by an officer of the court, who will serve as co-guardian with Mr. Muldoon for the two-month period. And I will receive a written report on Mr. LeBeck from that officer." Beckett's lips curved. "I think I'm going to enjoy this. Rehabilitation, Mr. Haridan, does not have to be accomplished in prison."

Rachel restrained herself from giving Haridan a smug grin. "Thank you, Your Honor."

"You're quite welcome, Counselor. Have your report to me every Friday afternoon, by three."

"My..." Rachel blinked, paled, then gaped. "My report? But, Your Honor, you can't mean for me to supervise Mr. LeBeck."

"That is precisely what I mean, Ms. Stanislaski. I believe having a male and a female authority figure will do our Mr. LeBeck a world of good."

"Yes, Your Honor, I agree. But . . . I'm not a social worker."

"You're a public servant, Ms. Stanislaski. So serve." She rapped her gavel. "Next case."

Stunned speechless by the judge's totally unorthodox ruling, Rachel moved to the back of the courtroom. "Good going, champ," her brother muttered in her ear. "Now you've got yourself hooked good."

"How could she do that? I mean, how could she just *do* that?"

"Everybody knows she's a little crazy." Furious, he swung Rachel out in the hall by an elbow. "There's no way in holy hell I'm letting you play baby-sitter for that punk. Beckett can't force you to."

"No, of course she can't." After dragging a hand through her hair, she shook Alex off. "Stop pulling at me and let me think."

"There's nothing to think about. You've got your own family and your own life. Watching over LeBeck is out of the question. And for all you know, that brother of his is just as dangerous. It's bad enough I have to watch you defend these creeps. No way I'm having you play big sister to one of them."

If he'd sympathized with her predicament, she might not have been quite as hasty. If he'd told her she'd gotten a raw deal, she probably would have agreed and set the wheels in motion to negate it. But...

"You don't have to watch me do anything, Alexi, and I can play big sister to whomever I choose. Now why don't you take that big bad badge of yours and go arrest some harmless vagrant.''

His blood boiled every bit as quickly as hers. ''You're not doing this.''

''I'll decide what I'm going to do. Now back off.''

He cupped a hand firmly on her chin just as she poked it out. ''I've got a good mind to—''

''The lady asked you to back off.'' Zack's voice was quiet, like a snake before it strikes. Alex whipped his head around, eyes hot and ready. It took all of his training to prevent himself from throwing the first punch.

''Keep out of our business.''

Zack planted his feet and prepared. ''I don't think so.''

They looked like two snarling dogs about to go for the throat. Rachel pushed her way between them.

''Stop it right now. This is no way to behave outside a courtroom. Muldoon, is this how you're going to show Nick responsibility? By picking fights?''

He didn't even glance at her, but kept his eyes on Alex. ''I don't like to see women pushed around.''

''I can take care of myself.'' She rounded on her brother. ''You're supposed to be a cop, for heaven's sake. And here you are acting like a rowdy schoolboy. You think about this. The court believes this is a viable solution, so I'm obligated to try it.''

''Damn it, Rachel—'' Alex's eyes went flat and cold when Zack stepped forward again. ''Pal, you mess with me, or my sister, you'll be wearing your teeth in a glass by your bedside.''

''Sister?'' Thoughtfully Zack examined one face, then the other. Oh, yes, the family resemblance was strong enough when you took a minute to study them. They both had those wild good looks that came through the blood. His anger cooled instantly. That changed things. He gave Rachel another speculative look. It changed a lot of things.

"Sorry. I didn't realize it was a family argument. You go ahead and yell at her all you want."

Alex had to fight to keep his lips from twitching. "All right, Rachel, you're going to listen to me."

She had to sigh. Then she had to take his face in her hands and kiss him. "Since when have I ever listened to you? Go away, Alexi. Chase some bad guys. And I'll have to take a rain check on that movie tonight."

There was no arguing with her. There never was. Changing tactics, Alex stared down Zack. "You watch out for her, Muldoon, and watch good. Because while you're at it, I'm going to be watching you."

"Sounds fair. Come by the bar anytime, Officer. First one's on the house."

Muttering under his breath, Alex stalked away. He turned once when Rachel called something out to him in Ukrainian. With a reluctant smile, he shook his head and kept walking.

"Translation?" Zack asked.

"Just that I would see him Sunday. Did you pay the bond?"

"Yeah, they're going to release him in a minute." Zack took a moment to reevaluate now that he realized she'd been kissing her brother that morning, not a lover. "I take it your brother isn't too thrilled to see you tangled up with me and Nick."

She gave Zack a long, bland look. "Who is, Muldoon? But since that's the court ruling, let's go get started."

"Get started?"

"We're going to pick up our charge, and you're going to move him into your apartment."

After spending the better part of a decade sharing close quarters with a couple hundred sailors. Zack gave one last wistful thought to the dissolution of his privacy. "Right." He took Rachel by the arm—a gesture she tried not to resent. "I don't suppose you've got any rope in that briefcase of yours."

It wasn't necessary to tie Nick up to gain his cooperation. But it was close. He sulked. He argued. He swore. By the time they'd walked out of the courthouse to hail a cab, Zack was biting down on fury and Nick had switched his resentment to Rachel.

"If this is the best deal you could cut, you'd better go back to law school. I've got rights, and the first one is to fire you."

"Your privilege, LeBeck," Rachel said, idly checking her watch. "You're certainly free to seek other counsel, but you can't fire me as your court-appointed guardian. We're stuck with each other for the next two months."

"That's bull. If you and that crazy judge think you can cook up—"

Zack made his move first, but Rachel merely elbowed him out of the way and went toe-to-toe with Nick. "You listen to me, you sorry, spoiled, sulky little jerk. You've got two choices—pretending to be a human being for the next eight weeks or going to prison for three years. I don't give a damn which way you go, but I'll tell you this. You think you're tough? You think you've got all the answers? You go inside for a week, and with that pretty face of yours the cons will be on you like dogs on fresh meat. You'd be willing to deal then, pal. Believe me, you'd be willing to deal.''

That shut him up, and Rachel had the added satisfaction of seeing his angry flush die to a sickly pallor. She gestured when a cab swung to the curb. ''Your choice, tough guy,'' she said, and turned to Zack. ''I've got work to do. I should be able to clear things up by around seven, then I'll be by to see how things are going.''

''I'll keep dinner warm,'' he said with a smirk, then caught her hand before she could walk away. ''Thanks. I mean it.'' She would have shrugged it off. His hand was hard as rock, calluses over calluses. He grinned. ''You're all right, Counselor. For a broad.'' He climbed into the cab behind his brother, sent her a quick salute as they pulled away. ''She's right about you being a jerk, Nick,'' Zack said easily. ''But you sure as hell picked a lawyer with first-class legs.''

Nick said nothing, but he did sneak a look out the rear window. He'd noticed Rachel's legs himself.

When they arrived at Nick's room ten minutes later, Zack had to swallow another bout of temper. It wouldn't do any good to yell at the kid every five minutes. But why in the hell had he picked such a neighborhood?

Hoods loitering on street corners. Drug deals negotiated out in broad daylight. Hookers already slicked up and stalking their prey. He could smell the stench of overripe garbage and unwashed humanity. His feet crunched on broken glass as they crossed the heaving sidewalk and entered the scarred and graffiti-laden brick building.

The smells were worse here, trapped inside, where even the fitful September breeze couldn't reach. Zack maintained his silence as they climbed up three floors, ignoring the shouted arguments behind closed doors and the occasional crash and weeping.

Nick unlocked the door and stepped into a single room furnished with a sagging iron bed, a broken dresser and a rickety wooden chair braced with a torn phone book. A few heavy-metal posters had been tacked to the stained walls in a pitiful attempt to give the room some personality. Helpless against the rage that geysered inside him, Zack let loose with a string of curses that turned the stale air blue.

"And what the hell have you been doing with the money I sent home every month when I was at sea? With the salary you were supposed to be earning from the delivery job? You're living in garbage, Nick. What's worse, you chose to live in it."

Not for a second would Nick have admitted that most of his money had gone into the Cobra treasury. Nor would he have admitted the shame he felt at having Zack see how he lived. "It's none of your damn business," he shot back. "This is my place, just like it's my life. You were never around, were you? Just because you got tired of cruising around on some stupid destroyer doesn't give you the right to come back here and take over."

"I've been back two years," Zack pointed out wearily. "And I spent a year of that watching the old man die. You didn't bother to come around much, did you?''

Nick felt a fresh wash of shame, and a deep, desperate sorrow that he was certain Zack could never understand. "He wasn't my old man."

Zack's head jerked up. Nick's hands fisted. Violent temper snapped and sizzled in the room. The slightest move would have sparked it into flame. Slowly, effortfully, Zack forced his body to relax.

"I'm not going to waste my time telling you he did the best he could."

"How the hell do you know?" Nick tossed back. "You weren't here. You got out your way, *bro*. I got out mine."

"Which brings us full circle. Pack up what you want, and let's go."

"This is my place—" Zack moved so quickly that the snarl caught in Nick's throat. He was up against the wall, Zack's big hands holding him in place while his thin body quivered with rage. Zack's face was so close to his, all Nick could see were those dark, dangerous eyes.

"For the next two months, like it or not, your place is with me. Now cut the crap and get some clothes together. Your free ride's over." He released Nick, knowing he had the strength and skill to snap his defiant young brother in half. "You got ten minutes, kid. You're working tonight."

By seven, Rachel was indulging a fantasy about a steamy bubble bath, a glass of crisp white wine and an hour with a good book. It helped ease the discomfort of the crowded subway car. She braced her feet against the swaying, kept her gaze focused on the middle distance. There were a few rough-looking characters scattered through the car whom she'd assessed and decided to ignore. A wino was snoring in the seat behind her, his face hidden under a newspaper.

At her stop, she bulled her way out, then started up the steps into the wet, windy evening. Hunched in her jacket, she fought with her umbrella, then slogged the two blocks to Lower the Boom.

The beveled glass door was heavy. She tugged it open and stepped out of the chill into the warmth, sounds and scents of an established neighborhood bar. It wasn't the dive she'd been expecting, but a wide wood-paneled room with a glossy mahogany bar trimmed in brass. The stools were burgundy leather, and every one was occupied. Neat tables were set around the room to accommodate more customers. There were the scents of whiskey and beer, cigarette smoke and grilled onions. A jukebox played the blues over the hum of conversation.

She spotted two waitresses winding their way through the patrons. No fishnet stockings and cleavage, Rachel mused. Both women were dressed in white slacks with modified sailor tops. There was a great deal of laughter, and she caught snatches of an argument as to whether the Mets still had a chance to make the play-offs.

Zack was in the center of the circular bar, drawing a beer for a customer. He'd exchanged his sweatshirt for a cable-knit turtleneck in navy blue. Oh, yes, she could see him on the deck of a ship, Rachel realized. Braced against the rolling, face to the wind. The bar's nautical theme, with its ship's bells and anchors, suited him.

She conjured up an image of him in uniform, found it entirely too attractive, and blinked it away.

She wasn't the fanciful type, she reminded herself. She was certainly no romantic. Above all, she was not the kind of woman who walked into a bar and found herself attracted to some land-locked sailor with shaggy hair, big shoulders and rough hands.

The only reason she was here was to uphold the court's ruling. However distasteful it might be to be hooked up with Zackary Muldoon for two months, she would do her duty.

But where was Nick?

"Would you like a table, miss?"

Rachel glanced around at a diminutive blonde hefting a large tray laden with sandwiches and beer. "No, thanks. I'll just go up to the bar. Is this place always crowded?"

The waitress's gray eyes brightened as she looked around the room. "Is it crowded? I didn't notice." With a laugh, she moved off while Rachel walked to the bar. She eased her way between two occupied stools, rested a foot on the brass rail and waited to catch Zack's eye.

"Well, darling..." The man on her left had a plump, pleasant face. He shifted on his stool to get a better look. "Don't think I've seen you in here before."

"No." Since he looked old enough to be her father, Rachel granted him a small smile. "You haven't."

"Pretty young girl like you shouldn't be here all alone." He leaned back—his stool creaking dangerously—and slapped the man on her other side on the shoulder. "Hey, Harry, we ought to buy this lady a drink."

Harry, who continued to sip his beer and work a crossword puzzle in the dim light, merely nodded. "Sure thing, Pete. Set it up. I need a five-letter word for the possibility of danger or pain."

Rachel glanced up. Zack was watching her, his blue eyes dark and steady, his bony face set and unsmiling. She felt something hot streak up her spine. *"Peril,"* she murmured, and fought off a shudder.

"Yeah! Hey, thanks!" Pleased, Harry pushed up his reading glasses and smiled at her. "First drink's on me. What'll you have, honey?"

"Pouilly-Fumé." Zack set a glass of pale gold wine in front of her. "And the first one's on the house." He lifted a brow. "That suit you, Counselor?"

"Yes." She let out the breath she hadn't been aware of holding. "Thank you."

"Zack always gets the prettiest ones," Pete said with a sigh. "Tip me another, kid. Least you can do, since you stole my girl." He shot Rachel a wink that had her relaxing with a smile again.

"And how often does he steal your girls, Pete?"

"Once, twice a week. It's humiliating." He grinned at Zack over a fresh beer. "Old Zack did date one of my girls once. Remember that time you were home on leave, Zack, you took my Rosemary to the movies, out to Coney Island? She's married and working on her second kid now."

Zack mopped up the bar with a cloth. "She broke my heart."

"There isn't a female alive who's scratched your heart, much less broken it." This from the blond waitress, who slapped an empty tray on the bar. "Two house wines, white. A Scotch, water back, and a draft. Harry, you ought to buy yourself one of those little clip-on lights before you ruin what's left of your eyes."

"*You* broke my heart, Lola." Zack put some glasses on the tray. "Why do you think I ran off and joined the navy?"

"Because you knew how good you'd look in dress whites." She laughed, hefted the tray, then glanced at Rachel. "You watch out for that one, sweetie. He's dangerous."

Rachel sipped at her wine and tried to pretend the scents slipping out from the kitchen weren't making her stomach rumble. "Have you got a minute?" she asked Zack. "I need to see where you're living."

Pete let out a hoot and rolled his eyes. "What's the guy got?" he wanted to know.

"More than you'll ever have." Zack grinned at him and signaled to another bartender to cover for him. "I just seem to attract aggressive women. Can't keep their hands off me."

Rachel finished off her wine before sliding from the stool. "I can restrain myself if I put my mind to it. Though it pains me to mar his reputation," she said to Pete, "I'm his brother's lawyer."

"No fooling?" Impressed, Pete took a closer look. "You the one who got the kid out of jail?"

"For the time being. Muldoon?"

"Right this way for the tour." He flipped up a section of the bar and stepped through. Again he took her arm. "Try to keep up."

"You know, I don't need you to hold on to me. I've been walking on my own for some time."

He pushed open a heavy swinging door that led to the kitchen. "I like holding on to you."

Rachel got the impression of gleaming stainless steel and white porcelain, the heavy scent of frying potatoes and grilling meat, before her attention was absorbed by an enormous man. He was dressed all in white, and his full apron was splattered and stained. Because he towered over Zack, Rachel estimated him at halfway to seven feet and a good three-fifty. If he'd played football, he would have been the entire defensive line.

His face was shiny from the kitchen heat, and the color of india ink. There was a scar running from one coal-black eye down to his massive chin. His hamlike hands were delicately building a club sandwich.

"Rio, this is Rachel Stanislaski, Nick's lawyer."

"How-de-do." She caught the musical cadence of the West Indies in his voice. "Got that boy washing dishes like a champ. Only broke him five or six all night."

Standing at a huge double sink, up to the elbows in soapy water, Nick turned his head and scowled. "If you call cleaning up someone else's slop a job, you can just—"

"Now don't you be using that language around this lady here." Rio picked up a cleaver and brought it down with a *thwack* to cut the sandwich in two, then four. "My mama always said nothing like washing dishes to give a body plenty of time for searching the soul. You keep washing and searching, boy."

Nick would have liked to have said more. Oh, he'd have loved to. But it was hard to argue with a seven-foot man holding a meat cleaver. He went back to muttering.

Rio smiled, and noted that Rachel was eyeing the sandwich. "How 'bout I fix you some hot meal? You can eat after you finish your business."

"Oh, I..." Her mouth was watering. "I really should get home."

"Zack, he's going to see you home after you're done. It's too late for a woman to go walking the streets by herself."

"I don't need—"

"Dish her up some of your chili, Rio," Zack suggested as he pulled Rachel toward a set of stairs. "This won't take long."

Rachel found herself trapped, hip to hip with him in a narrow staircase. He smelled of the sea, she realized, of that salty, slightly electric scent that meant a storm was brewing beyond the horizon. "It's very kind of you to offer, Muldoon, but I don't need a meal, or an escort."

"You'll get both, need them or not." He turned, effectively trapping her against the wall. It felt good to have his body brush hers. As good as he'd imagined it would. "I never argue with Rio. I met him in Jamaica about six years ago—in a little bar tussle. I watched him pick up a two-hundred-pound man and toss him through a wall. Now, Rio's mostly a peaceful sort of man, but if you get him riled, there's no telling what he might do." Zack lifted a hand and wound a lock of Rachel's hair around his finger. "Your hair's wet."

She slapped his hand away and tried to pretend her heart wasn't slamming in her throat. "It's raining."

"Yeah. I can smell it on you. You sure are something to look at, Rachel."

She couldn't move forward, couldn't move back, so she did the only thing open to her. She bristled like a cornered cat. "You're in my way, Muldoon. My advice is to move your butt and save the Irish charm for someone who'll appreciate it."

"In a minute. Was that Russian you yelled after your brother today?"

"Ukrainian," she said between her teeth.

"Ukrainian." He considered that, and her. "I never made it to the Soviet Union."

She lifted a brow. "Neither have I. Now can we save this discussion until after I've seen the living arrangements?"

"All right." He started up the steps again, his hand on the small of her back. "It's not much, but I can guarantee it's a large step up from the dump Nick was living in. I don't know why he—" He cut himself off and shrugged. "Well, it's done."

Rachel had a feeling it was just beginning.

Chapter Three

Though it brought on all manner of headaches, Rachel took her new charge seriously. She could handle the inconvenience, the extra time sliced out of her personal life, Nick's surly and continued resentment. What gave her the most trouble was the enforced proximity with Zackary Muldoon.

She couldn't dismiss him and she couldn't work around him. Having to deal with him on what was essentially a day-to-day basis was sending her stress level through the roof.

If only she could pigeonhole him, she thought as she walked from the subway to her apartment after a Sunday dinner with her family, it would somehow make things easier. But after nearly a week of trying, she hadn't even come close.

He was rough, impatient, and, she suspected, potentially violent. Yet he was concerned enough about his stepbrother to shell out money and—much more vital—time and energy to set the boy straight. In his off hours, he dressed in clothes more suited to the rag basket than his tall, muscled frame. Yet when she'd walked through his apartment over the bar, she'd found everything neat as a pin. He was always putting his hands on her—her arm, her hair, her shoulder—but he had yet to make the kind of move she was forever braced to repel.

He flirted with his female customers, but as far as Rachel had been able to glean, it stopped at flirtation. He'd never been married, and though he'd left his family for months, even years, at a time, he'd given up the sea and had landlocked himself when his father became too ill to care for himself.

He irritated her on principle. But on some deeper, darker level, the very things about him that irritated her fanned little flames in her gut that Rachel could only describe as pure lust.

She'd tried to cool them by reminding herself that she wasn't the lusty type. Passionate, yes. When it came to her work, her family and her ambitions. But men, though she enjoyed their companionship and their basic maleness, had never been at the top of her list of priorities.

Sex was even lower than that. And it was very annoying to find herself itchy.

So who was Zackary Muldoon, and would she be better off not knowing?

When he stepped out of the shadows into the glow of a streetlight, she jolted and choked back a scream.

"Where the hell have you been?"

"I— Damn it, you scared me to death." She brought a trembling hand back out of her purse, where it had shot automatically toward a bottle of Mace. Oh, she hated to be frightened. Detested having to admit she could be vulnerable. "What are you doing lurking out here in front of my building?"

"Looking for you. Don't you ever stay home?"

"Muldoon, with me it's party, party, party." She stalked up the steps and jammed her key in the outer door. "What do you want?"

"Nick took off."

She stopped halfway through the door, and he bumped solidly into her. "What do you mean, took off?"

"I mean he slipped out of the kitchen sometime this afternoon, when Rio wasn't looking. I can't find him." He was so furious—with Nick, with Rachel, with himself—that it took all of his control not to punch his fist through the wall. "I've been at it almost five hours, and I can't find him."

"All right, don't panic." Her mind was already clicking ahead as she walked through the tiny lobby to the single gate-fronted elevator. "It's early, just ten o'clock. He knows his way around."

"That's the trouble." Disgusted with himself, Zack stepped in the car with her. "He knows his way around too well. The rule was, he'd tell me when he was going, and where. I've got to figure he's hanging out with the Cobras."

"Nick's not going to break that kind of tie overnight." Rachel continued to think as the elevator creaked its way up to the fourth floor. "We can drive ourselves crazy running around the city trying to hunt him down, or we can call in the cavalry."

"The cavalry?"

She shoved the gate open and walked into the hallway. "Alex."

"No cops," Zack said quickly, grabbing her arms. "I'm not setting the cops on him."

"Alex isn't just a cop. He's my brother." Struggling to hold on to her own patience, she pried his fingers from her arms. "And I'm an officer of the court, Zack. If Nick's breaking the provisions, I can't ignore it."

"I'm not going to see him tossed back in a cell barely a week after I got him out."

"*We* got him out," she corrected, then unlocked her door. "If you didn't want my help and advice, you shouldn't have come."

Zack shrugged and stepped inside. "I guess I figured we could go out looking together."

The room was hardly bigger than the one Nick had rented, but it was all female. Not flouncy, Zack thought. Rachel wouldn't go for flounce. There were vivid colors in the plump pillows tossed over a low-armed sofa. The scented candles were burned down to various lengths, and mums were just starting to fade in a china vase.

There was a huge bronze-framed oval mirror on one wall. Its glass needed resilvering. A three-foot sculpture in cool white marble dominated one corner. It reminded Zack of a mermaid rising up out of the sea. There were smaller sculptures, as well, all of them passionate, some of them bordering on the ferocious. A timber wolf rearing out of a slab of oak, twisted fingers of bronze and copper that looked like a fire just out of control, a smooth and sinuous malachite cobra ready to strike.

There were shelves of books, and dozens of framed photographs—and there was the unmistakable scent of woman.

Zack felt uncharacteristically awkward and clumsy, and completely out of place. He stuck his hands in his pockets, certain he'd knock over one of those slender tapers. His mother had liked candles, he remembered. Candles and flowers and blue china bowls.

"I'll make coffee." Rachel tossed her purse aside and walked into the adjoining kitchen.

"Yeah. Good." Restless, Zack roamed the room, checked out the view through the cheerful striped curtains, frowned over the photographs that were obviously of her family, paced back to the sofa. "I don't know what I'm doing. What makes me think I can play daddy to a kid Nick's age? I wasn't around for half his life. He hates me. He's got a right."

"You've been doing fine," Rachel countered, taking out cups and saucers. "You're not playing daddy, you're being his brother. If you weren't around for half his life, it's because you had a life of your own. And he doesn't hate you. He's angry and full of resentment which is a long way from hate—which he wouldn't have any right to. Now stop feeling sorry for yourself, and get out the milk."

"Is that how you cross-examine?" Not sure whether he was amused or annoyed, Zack opened the refrigerator.

"No, I'm much tougher than that in court."

"I bet." He shook his head at the contents of her refrigerator. Yogurt, a package of bologna, another of cheese, several diet soft drinks, a jug of white wine, two eggs, and half a stick of butter. "You're out of milk."

She swore, then sighed. "So we drink it black. Did you and Nick have a fight?"

"No— I mean no more than usual. He snarls, I snarl back. He swears, I swear louder. But we actually had what could pass for a conversation last night, then watched an old movie on the tube after the bar closed."

"Ah, progress..." She handed him his coffee in a dainty cup and saucer that felt like a child's tea set in his hands.

"We get a lot of families in for lunch on Sundays." Zack ignored the china handle and wrapped his fingers around the bowl of the cup. "He was down in the kitchen at noon. I figured he might like to knock off early, you know, take some time for himself. I went into the kitchen around four. Rio didn't want to rat on him, so he'd been covering for him for an hour or so. I hoped he'd just taken a breather, but... Then I went out looking." Zack finished off the coffee, then helped himself to more. "I've been pretty hard on him the last few days. It seemed like the best way. On my first ship, my CO was a regular Captain Bligh. I hated the bastard until I realized he'd turned us into a crew." Zack grinned a little. "Hell, I still hated him, but I never forgot him."

"Stop beating yourself up." She couldn't prevent herself from reaching out, touching his arm. "It isn't as if you hanged him from the yardarm or whatever. Now sit down and try to relax. Let me talk to Alex."

He did sit, though he wasn't happy about it. Because he felt like an idiot trying to balance the delicate saucer on his knee, he set it down on the table. There wasn't an ashtray in sight, so he clamped down on the urge for a cigarette.

He paid little attention to Rachel until her voice rose in frustration. Then he smiled a little. She was certainly full of fire, punching out requests and orders with the aplomb of a seasoned seaman. Lord, he'd gotten so he looked forward to hearing that throaty, impatient voice. How many times over the past few days had he made up excuses to call her?

Too many, he admitted. Something about the lady had hooked him, and Zack wasn't sure whether he wanted to pry himself loose or be reeled in.

And the last thing he should be doing now was thinking of his libido, he reminded himself. He had to think about Nick.

Obviously Rachel's brother was resisting, but she wasn't taking no for an answer. When she switched to heated Ukrainian, Zack reached over to toy with the spitting cobra in the center of the coffee table. It drove him crazy when she talked in Ukrainian.

"Tak," she said, satisfied that she'd worn Alex down. "I owe you one, Alexi." She laughed, a rich, and full-blooded laugh that sent heat straight to Zack's midsection. "All right, all right, so I'll owe you two." Zack watched her hang up and cross long legs covered in a hunter-green material that was silky enough to whisper seductively when her thighs brushed together. "Alex and his partner are going to cruise around, check out some of the Cobras' known haunts. They'll let us know if they see him."

"So we wait?"

"We wait." She rose and took a fresh legal pad from a drawer. "To pass the time, you can fill me in a little more on Nick's background. You said his mother died when he was about fifteen. What about his father?"

"His mother wasn't married before." Zack reached automatically for a cigarette, then remembered. Recognizing the gesture, Rachel rose again and found a chipped ashtray. "Thanks." Relieved, he lit a cigarette, cupping his fingers around the tip out of habit. "Nadine was about eighteen when she got pregnant, and the guy wasn't interested in family. He took off and left her to fend for herself. So she had Nick and did what she could. One day she came into the bar looking for work. Dad hired her."

"How old was Nick?"

"Four or five. Nadine was barely making ends meet. Sometimes she couldn't get a sitter for him, so Dad told her to bring the kid along and I'd watch him. He was okay," Zack said with a half smile. "I mean, he was real quiet. Most of the time he'd just watch you like he was expecting to get dumped on. But he was smart. He'd just started school, but he could already read, and he could print some, too. Anyway, a couple months later, Nadine and my father got married. Dad was about twenty years older than she was, but I guess they were both lonely. My mother'd been dead for more than ten years. Nadine and the kid moved in."

"How did you...how did Nick adjust?"

"It seemed okay. Hell, I was a kid myself." Restless again, he rose to pace. "Nadine bent over backward trying to please everyone. That's the way she was. My father...he wasn't always easy, you know, and he put a lot of time into the bar. We weren't a Norman Rockwell kind of family, but we did okay." He glanced back at her photographs, surprised at the quick twinge of envy. "I didn't mind the kid hanging around me. Much. Then I joined the navy, right out of high school. It was kind of a family tradition. When

Nadine died, it was hard on Nick. Hard on my father. I guess you could say they took it out on each other.''

"Is that when Nick started to get into trouble?"

"I'd say he got into his share before that, but it got worse. Whenever I'd get back, my father would be full of complaints. The boy wouldn't do this, he did that. He was hanging around with punks. He was looking for trouble. And Nick would skulk off or slam out. If I said anything, he'd tell me to kiss his—'' He shrugged. "You get the picture.''

She thought she did. A young boy unwanted by his father. He begins to admire his new brother, and then feels deserted by him, as well. He loses his mother and finds himself alone with a man old enough to be his grandfather, a man who couldn't relate to him.

Nothing permanent in his life—except rejection.

"I'm not a psychologist, Zack, but I'd say he needs time to trust that you mean to stay part of his life this time around. And I don't think taking a firm hand is wrong. In fact, I think that's just what he'd understand from you, and respect in the long run. Maybe that just needs to be balanced a bit.'' She sighed and set her notes aside. "Which is where I come in. So far, I've been just as rough on him. Let's try a little good-cop-bad-cop. I'll be the sympathetic ear. Believe me, I understand hotheads and bad boys. I grew up with them. We can start by—'' The phone rang and she snagged it. "Hello. Uh-huh. Good. That's good. Thanks, Alex.'' She could see the relief in Zack's eyes before she hung up. "They spotted him on his way back to the bar.''

Relief sparked quickly into anger. "When I get my hands on him—''

"You'll ask, in a very reasonable fashion, where he was," Rachel told him. "And to make certain you do, I'm going with you."

Nick let himself into Zack's apartment. He figured he'd been pretty clever. He'd managed to slip in and out of the kitchen without setting off Rio's radar. The way they were watching him around here, he thought, he might as well be doing time.

Everything was going wrong, anyway. He ducked into the kitchen and, since Zack wasn't around to say any different, opened a beer. He'd just wanted to check in with the guys, see what was happening on the street.

And they'd treated him like an outsider.

They didn't trust him, Nick thought resentfully as he swigged one long swallow, then two. Reece had decided that since he'd gotten out so quickly, he must have ratted. He thought he'd convinced most of the gang that he was clean, but when he'd spilled the whole story—from how he'd been caught to how he'd ended up washing dishes in Zack's bar, they'd laughed at him.

It hadn't been the good, communal laughter he'd shared with the Cobras in the past. It had been snide and nasty, with T.J. giggling like a fool and Reece smirking and playing with his switchblade. Only Cash had been the least bit sympathetic, saying how it was a raw deal.

Not one of them had bothered to explain why they'd left him hanging when the cop showed up.

When he'd left them, he'd gone by Marla's place. They'd been seeing each other steadily for the past couple of months, and he'd been sure he'd find a sympathetic ear, and a nice warm body. But she'd been out—with somebody else.

Looked as though he'd been dumped again, all around. Nothing new, Nick told himself. But the sting of rejection wasn't any easier to take this time.

Damn it, they were supposed to be his family. They were supposed to stick up for him, stand by him, not shake him loose at the first hint of trouble. He wouldn't have done it to them, he told himself, and heaved the empty beer bottle into the trash, where it smashed satisfactorily. No, by God, he wouldn't have done it to them.

When he heard the door open, he set his face into bored lines and sauntered out of the kitchen. He'd expected Zack, but he hadn't expected Rachel. Nick felt a heat that was embarrassment and something more try to creep up into his cheeks.

Zack peeled off his jacket, hoping he had a firm grip on his temper. "I guess you've got a good reason why you skipped out this afternoon."

"I wanted some air." Nick pulled out a cigarette, struck a match. "There a law against it?"

"We had an agreement," Zack said evenly. "You were supposed to check with me before you went out, and tell me your plans."

"No, man. You had an agreement. Last I looked it was a free country and people could go for a walk when they felt like it." He gestured toward Rachel. "You bring the lawyer to sue me, or what?"

"Listen, kid—"

"I'm not a kid," Nick shot back. "You came and went as you damn well pleased when you were my age."

"I wasn't a thief at your age." Incensed, Zack took two steps forward. Rachel snagged his arm.

"Why don't you go down and get me a glass of wine, Muldoon? The kind you served me the other night will do just fine." When he tried to shake her off, she tightened her grip. "I want a moment alone with my client, so take your time."

"Fine." He bit off the word before he stalked to the door. "Whatever she says, pal, you're on double KP next week. And if you try to sneak off again, I'll have Rio chain you to the sink." He gave himself the sweet satisfaction of slamming the door.

Nick took another puff on his cigarette and dropped onto the couch. "Big talk," he muttered. "He's always figured he could boss me around. I've been on my own for years, and it's time he got that straight."

Rachel sat down beside him. She didn't bother to mention that she could smell the beer on his breath and he was underage. Why hadn't Zack seen the raw need in Nick's eyes? Why hadn't *she* seen it before?

"It's tough, having to move in here after having a place of your own."

Her voice was mild, and without censure. Nick squinted through the smoke. "Yeah," he said, cautiously. "I can hack it for a couple of months, I guess."

"When I first moved out, I was a little older than you—not much. I was excited, and scared, and lonely. I wouldn't have admitted to lonely if my life had depended on it. I've got two older brothers. They checked up on me constantly." She laughed a little. Nick didn't crack a smile. "It infuriated me, and it made me feel safe. They still get on my back, but I can usually find a way around them."

Nick stared hard at the tip of his cigarette. "He's not my real brother."

Oh, Lord, he looked young, she thought. And so terribly sad. "I suppose that would depend on your definition of real." She laid a hand on his knee, prepared for him to shrug her off, but he only switched his gaze from his cigarette to her fingers. "It'd be easier for you to believe he doesn't care, but you're not stupid, Nick."

There was a hot ball in his throat that he refused to believe was tears. "Why should he care? I'm nothing to him."

"If he didn't care, he wouldn't yell at you so much. Take it from me—I come from a family where a raised voice is a sign of unswerving love. He wants to look out for you."

"I can look out for myself."

"And have been," she agreed. "But most of us can use a hand now and again. He won't thank me for telling you all this, but I think you should know." She waited until he raised his eyes again. "He's had to take out a loan to pay for the stolen property and the damages."

"That's bull," Nick shot back, appalled. "Did he lay that trip on you?"

"No, I checked on it myself. It seems old Mr. Muldoon's illness drained quite a bit of his savings, and Zack's. Zack's gotten the bar back on a pretty solid footing again, but he didn't have enough to swing the costs. A man doesn't put himself out like that for someone he doesn't care about."

The sick feeling in Nick's gut had him crushing out the cigarette. "He just feels obligated, that's all."

"Maybe. Either way, it seems to me you owe him something, Nick. At least you owe him a little cooperation over the next few weeks. He was scared when he came looking for me tonight. You probably don't want to believe that, either."

"Zack's never been scared of anything."

"He didn't come right out and say it, but I think he believed you'd taken off for good, that he wasn't going to see you again."

"Where the hell would I go?" he demanded. "There's nobody—" He broke off, ashamed to admit there was no one to go to. "We made a deal," he muttered, "I'm not going to skip."

"I'm glad to hear it. And I'm not going to ask you where you went," she added with a faint smile. "If I did, I'd have to put it in my report to Judge Beckett, and I'd rather not. So we'll just say you went out for some air, lost track of the time. Maybe the next time you feel like you've got to get out, you could call me."

"Why?"

"Because I know how it feels when you need to break loose." He looked so lost that Rachel skimmed a hand through his hair, brushing it back from his face. "Lighten up, Nick. It's not a crime to be friends with your lawyer, either. So what do you say? You give me a break and try a little harder to get along with Zack, and I'll do what I can to keep him off your back? I know all kinds of tricks for handling nosy older brothers."

Her scent was clouding his senses. He didn't know why he hadn't noticed before how beautiful her eyes were. How deep and wide and soft. "Maybe you and I could go out sometime."

"Sure." She saw the suggestion only as a break-through in trust, and she smiled. "Rio's a terrific cook, but once in a while you just got to have pizza, right?"

"Yeah. So I can call you?"

"Absolutely." She gave his hand a quick squeeze. When his hand tightened over hers, she was only mildly surprised. Before she could comment, Zack was pushing the door open again. Nick jumped up as if he were on a string.

Zack passed Rachel her wine, then handed Nick the ginger-ale bottle he had hooked under one finger. Taking his time, he twisted off the top of the beer he had hooked under another. "So, did you two finish your consultation?"

"For now." Rachel sipped her wine and lifted a brow at Nick.

It wasn't easy, especially after what she'd told him Zack had done, but Nick met his brother's eyes. "I'm sorry I took off."

The surprise was so great that Zack had to swallow quickly or choke on his beer. "Okay. We can work out a schedule so you can have more free time." What the hell did he do now? "Uh . . . Rio could use some help swabbing down the kitchen. Things usually break up early on Sunday nights."

"Sure, no problem." Nick started for the door. "See you, Rachel."

When the door closed, Zack dropped down beside her, shaking his head. "What'd you do, hypnotize him?"

"Not exactly."

"Well, what the hell did you say to him?"

She sighed, tremendously pleased with herself, and settled back. "That's privileged information. He just needs someone to stroke his bruised ego now and again. You two may not be biological brothers, but your temperament's very similar."

"Oh." He settled back, as well, swinging an arm around the top of the couch so that he could play with her hair. "How's that."

"You're both hotheaded and stubborn—which is easy for me to recognize, as I come from a long line of the same." Enjoying the wine and the quiet, she let her eyes close. "You don't like to admit you made a mistake, and you'd rather punch your way out of a problem than reason it through."

"Are you trying to say those are faults?"

She had to laugh. "We'll just call them personality traits. My family is ripe with passionate natures. And what a passionate nature requires is an outlet. My sister Natasha had dance, then her own business and her family. My brother Mikhail has his art. Alexi has his quest to right wrongs, and I have the law. As I see it, you had the navy, and now this bar. Nick hasn't found his yet."

He brushed a finger lightly over the nape of her neck, felt the quick quiver that ran through her. "Do you really consider the law enough of an outlet for passion?"

"The way I play it." She opened her eyes, but the smile that had started to curve her lips died away. He'd shifted, and his face was close—much too close—and his hands had slipped down to her shoulders. The warning bell that rang in her brain had come too late. "I've got to get home," she said quickly. "I've got a nine-o'clock hearing."

"I'll take you in a minute."

"I know the way, Muldoon."

"I'll take you," he said again, and something in his tone made it quite clear that he wasn't talking about walking her to her door. He tugged the wineglass out of her hand and set it aside. "We were talking about passionate natures." His fingers skimmed up through her hair, fisted in it. "And outlets."

In an automatic defensive gesture, her hand slammed against his chest, but he continued to draw her closer. "I came here to help you, Muldoon," she reminded him as his mouth hovered dangerously above hers. "Not to play games."

"Just testing your theory, Counselor." He nipped lightly at her lower lip, once, twice. When that teasing sample stirred the juices, he crushed his mouth to hers and devoured.

She could stop him. Of course she would stop him, Rachel told herself. She knew how to defend herself against unwanted advances. The trouble was, she hadn't a clue as to how to defend herself against advances she didn't want to want.

His mouth was so... avid. So impatient. So greedy. She wondered if he would swallow her whole. He used lips and tongue and teeth devastatingly. If there was an instant, some fraction of a heartbeat, when she could have resisted, it passed unnoticed, and she was swamped by the hot wave that was his need, or hers. Or what they made together. On one long, throaty moan, she went under for the third time, dragging him with her.

He'd been prepared for her to slap or scratch. And he would have accepted it, would have forced himself to be satisfied with that quick, tempting taste. He was

a man with large appetites, but he had never been one
to take what wasn't offered willingly.

She didn't offer. She exploded. In that blink of time
before his mouth covered hers, he'd seen the fire come
into her eyes, that dark, liquid fire that equaled passion. When the kiss had gone from teasing to fevered,
she had answered, pulling him far deeper into that hot
well of desires than he'd intended to go.

And that moan. It sprinted along his spine, that
glorious feline sound that was both surrender and demand. Even as it died away, she was wrapping herself
around him, pressing that incredibly lean and limber
body against his in a way that had a chain of explo-
sions rioting through his system.

She heard his breathy oath, felt the long cushions of
the couch press into her back as he shifted her. For one
wild moment, all she could think was Yes! This was
what she wanted, this wild flurry of sensations, this
crazed, mindless mating of flesh. As his mouth raced
down to savage her throat, she arched against him,
craving the possession.

Then he said her name. Groaned it. The shock of
hearing it ripped her back to reality. She was grap-
pling on a couch in a strange apartment with a man
she barely knew.

"No." His hands were moving over her, and they
nearly dragged her back into the whirlwind. Desperate to pull away, she shoved and struggled. "Stop. I
said no."

He couldn't get his breath. If someone had held a
gun to his head, he wouldn't have moved. But the *no*
stopped him. He managed to lift his head, and the
reckless light in his eyes had her fighting against a
shudder. "Why?"

"Because this is insane." God, she could still taste him on her lips, and the churning for more of him was making her crazy. "Get off me."

He could have strangled her for making him want to beg. "Your call, lady." Because his hands were unsteady, he balled them into fists. "I thought you said you didn't play games."

She was humiliated, furious, and frustrated beyond belief. As she saw it, the best disguise was full-blown anger. "I don't. You're the one who pushed yourself on me. The simple fact is, I'm not interested."

"I guess that's why you were kissing me so hard my teeth are loose."

"You kissed me." She jabbed a finger at him. "And you're so damn big I couldn't stop you."

"A simple no did," he reminded her, and lit a cigarette. "Let's keep it honest, Counselor. I wanted to kiss you. I've been wanting to do that, and more, ever since I saw you sitting like a queen in that grubby station house. Now, maybe you didn't feel the same way, but when I kissed you, you kissed me right back."

Sometimes retreat was the best defense. Rachel snatched up her purse and jacket. "It's done, so there's nothing more to discuss."

"Wrong." He was up and blocking her path. "We can finish discussing it while I take you home."

"I don't want you to take me home. I'm not having you take me home." Eyes blazing, she swung her jacket over her shoulders. "And if you insist on following me there, I'll have you arrested for harassment."

He merely grabbed her by the arm. "Try it."

She did something she wished she'd done the first time she laid eyes on him. She punched him in the stomach. He let out a little *whoosh* of air, and his eyes narrowed.

"First one's free. Now, we can walk to the subway, or I can carry you there."

"What's wrong with you?" she shouted. "Can't you take no for an answer?"

His response was to shove her back against the door and kiss the breath out of her. "If I didn't," he said between his teeth, "we wouldn't be walking out of here right now when you've got me so wound up I'm going to have to live in a cold shower for the next week." He yanked open the door. "Now... are you going to walk, or are you going to ride over my shoulder?"

She stuck out her chin and sailed past him.

She'd walk, all right. But she'd be damned if she'd speak to him.

Chapter Four

At the end of a harried ten-hour day, Rachel walked out of the courthouse. She should have been feeling great—her last client was certainly happy with the non-guilty verdict she'd gotten for him. But this time the victory hadn't managed to lift her spirits. The only solution she could see was to pick up a quart of ice cream on the way home and gorge herself into a sugar coma.

It usually worked, and since, as a law-abiding citizen, she couldn't relieve her tension by striding into Lower the Boom and shooting Zackary Muldoon through his thick skull, it was the safest alternative.

She almost tripped over her own feet when she saw him rise from his perch at the bottom of the steps.

"Counselor." He reached out a hand when she teetered. "Steady as she goes."

"What now?" she demanded, jerking away. "Doesn't it occur to you that—even though I've been appointed by the court as Nick's co-guardian—I'm entitled to an hour of personal time without you in my face?"

He studied that face, noting signs of fatigue, as well as temper, in those big, tawny eyes. "You know, honey, I figured you'd be in a better mood after winning a case like you just did. Let's try these." With a flourish, he brought his other hand from behind his back. It was filled with gold, bronze and rust-colored mums.

Refusing to be charmed, Rachel gave them one long, suspicious glare. "What are those for?"

"To replace the ones that are dying in your apartment." When she made no move to take them, he bit down on his impatience. He'd come to apologize, damn it, and it looked as though she was going to make him go through with it. "Okay, I'm sorry. I got pushy the other night. And after I got over wanting to choke you, I realized you'd gone out of your way to do me a favor, and I'd repaid it by..." Furious all over again, he thrust the flowers at her. "Hell, lady, all I did was kiss you."

All he did? she thought, tempted to toss the flowers down and grind them underfoot. Just kissing didn't jangle a woman's system for better than thirty-six hours. "Why don't you take your flowers, and your charming apology, and—"

"Hold on." He thought it better to stop her before she said something he'd regret. "I said I was sorry, and I meant it, but maybe I should be more specific." To ensure that she'd stay put until he was finished, he wrapped his fingers around the lapel of her plum-colored jacket. "I'm not sorry I kissed you, any more than I'm going to be sorry the next time I kiss you. I am sorry for the way I acted after you put on the brakes."

She lifted a brow. "The way you acted," she repeated. "You mean like a jerk."

It gave her a great deal of pleasure to see a muscle twitch in his jaw.

"Okay."

A smart attorney knew when to accept a compromise. Lips pursed, she studied the flowers. "Are these a bribe, Muldoon?"

The way she said his name, with just a hint of a sneer, told him he'd gotten over the first hurdle. "Yeah."

"All right, I'll take them."

"Gee, thanks." Now that his hands were free, he tucked his thumbs in his front pockets. "I slipped in the courtroom about an hour ago and watched you."

"Oh?" She couldn't tell him how glad she was she hadn't seen him. "And?"

"Not bad. Turning a vandalism charge around on the other guy—"

"The plaintiff," she explained. "My client was justifiably frustrated after he'd exhausted all reasonable attempts to have his landlord live up to the terms of his lease."

"And spray painting The Landlord from Hell all over the guy's brownstone on the Upper West Side was his way of relieving that frustration."

"He certainly made his point. My client had paid his rent on time and in good faith, and the landlord consistently refused to acknowledge each and every request for repair and maintenance. Under the terms of the lease—''

"Hey, babe." Zack raised a hand, palm out. "You don't have to sell me. By the time you got through, I was pulling for him. There were murmurs in the visitors' gallery about lynching the landlord." His mouth was sober enough, but his eyes danced with humor. The contrast was all but irresistible.

Her smile was quick and wicked. "I love justice."

Reaching out, he toyed with the tiny gold links circling her neck. "Maybe you'd like to celebrate your victory for the underdog. Want to go for a walk?"

Mistake. The word popped full-blown into her mind, but she could smell the spicy flowers, and the evening was beautifully balmy. "I guess I would, as long as it's to my apartment. I should put these in water."

"Let me take that." He'd tugged the briefcase out of her hand before she could object. Then—she should have expected it—he took her arm. "What do you carry in here, bricks?"

"The law's a weighty business, Muldoon." His grip on her forced her to slow her pace to his. He strolled when she would have strode. "So, how's it going with Nick?"

"It's better. At least I think it's better. He balked at the idea of Rio teaching him to cook, but the idea of busing tables didn't seem to bother him much. He still won't talk to me—I mean really talk to me. But it's only been a week."

"You've got seven more."

"Yeah." He let go of her arm long enough to reach into his pocket and take out a handful of change. He dropped it into a panhandler's cup in a gesture so automatic that Rachel assumed he made a habit of it. "I figure if they could turn me from a green recruit into a sailor in about the same amount of time, I have a pretty good shot at this."

"Do you miss it?" She tilted her head up to his. "Being at sea?"

"Not so much anymore. Sometimes I still wake up at night and think I'm aboard ship." Then there were the nightmares, but that wasn't something a man shared with a woman. "Once things are stable, I'm planning on buying a boat, maybe taking a couple of months and sailing down to the Islands. Maybe a nice ketch, forty-two feet—not too fancy." He could already see it, a trim little honey, quick to the touch, brass and mahogany gleaming, white sails bulging in the wind. He imagined Rachel would look just fine standing at the bow. "You ever done any sailing?"

"Not unless you count taking the ferry over to Liberty Island."

"You'd like it." He skimmed his fingers lightly down her arm. "It's what you might call an outlet."

Rachel decided it was safer not to comment. When they reached her building, she turned to him, holding out a hand for her briefcase. "Thanks for the flowers, and the walk. I'll probably come by the bar tomorrow after work and look in on Nick."

Instead of giving her the briefcase, he closed his hand over hers. "I took the night off, Rachel. I want to spend it with you."

Her quick jolt of alarm both pleased and amused him. "Excuse me?"

"Maybe I should rephrase that. I'd like to spend the night with you—several nights running, in fact—but I'll settle for the evening." He managed to wind a lock of her hair around his finger before she remembered to bat his hand away. "Some food, some music. I know a place that does both really well. If the idea of a date makes you nervous..."

"I'm not nervous." Not exactly, she thought.

"Anyway, we can consider it a few hours between two people who have a mutual interest. It couldn't hurt if we got to know each other a little better." He pulled out his trump card. "For Nick's sake."

She studied him, much as she had the witness she'd so ruthlessly cross-examined earlier. "You want to spend the evening with me for Nick's sake?"

Giving up, he grinned. "Hell, no. There's bound to be some spillover benefit there, but I want to spend the evening with you for purely selfish reasons."

"I see. Well, since you didn't perjure yourself, I may be able to cut a deal. It has to be an early evening, somewhere I can dress comfortably. And you won't..." How had he phrased it? "Get pushy."

"You're a tough one, Counselor."

"You got it."

"Deal," he said, and gave her the briefcase.

"Fine. Come back in twenty minutes. I'll be ready."

A bar, Rachel thought a half hour later. She should have known Zack would spend his night off on a busman's holiday. Actually, she supposed it was more of a club. There was a three-piece band playing the blues on a small raised stage, and there were a handful of couples dancing on a tiny square of floor surrounded by tables. From the way he was greeted by the waitress, he was obviously no stranger.

Within moments they were settled at a table in a shadowy corner, with a glass of wine for her and a mug of beer for him.

"I come for the music," he explained. "But the food's good, too. That's not something I mention to Rio."

"Since I've seen the way he slices a club sandwich, I can't hold that against you." She squinted at the tiny menu. "What do you recommend?"

"Trust me." His thigh brushed hers as he shifted closer to toy with the stones dangling at her ear. He smiled at her narrowed eyes. "And try the grilled chicken."

She discovered he could be trusted, at least when it came to food. Enjoying every bite, lulled by the music, she began to relax. "You said the navy was a family tradition. Is that why you joined, really?"

"I wanted to get out." He nursed a second beer, appreciating the way she plowed through the meal. He'd always been attracted to a woman with an appetite. "I wanted to see the world. I only figured on the four years, but then I re-upped."

"Why?"

"I got used to being part of a crew, and I liked the life. Looking out and seeing nothing but water, or watching the land pull away when you headed out. Coming into port and seeing a place you'd never seen before."

"In nearly ten years I imagine you saw a lot of places."

"The Mediterranean, the South Pacific, the Indian Ocean, the Persian Gulf. Froze my...fingers off in the North Atlantic and watched sharks feed in the Coral Sea."

Both fascinated and amused, she propped her elbows on the table. "Did you know you didn't mention one land mass? Doesn't one body of water look pretty much like another from the deck of a ship?"

"No." He didn't think he could explain, knew he wasn't lyrical enough to describe the varying hues of the water, the subtle degrees of the power of the deep. What it felt like to watch dolphins run, or whales sound. "I guess you could say that a body of water has its own personality, just like a body of land does."

"You do miss it."

"It gets in your blood. How about you? Is the law a Stanislaski family tradition?"

"No." Under the table, her foot began to tap to the beat of the bass. "My father's a carpenter. So was his father."

"Why law?"

"Because I'd grown up in a family who'd known oppression. They escaped Ukraine with what they could carry in a wagon—in the winter through the mountains—eventually reaching Austria. I was born here, the first of my family to be born here."

"It sounds as though you regret it."

He was astute, she decided. More astute than she'd given him credit for. "I suppose I regret not being a part of both sides. They haven't forgotten what it was like to taste freedom for the first time. I've never known anything but freedom. Freedom and justice go hand in hand.''

"Some might say you could be serving justice in a nice, cushy law firm.''

"Some might.''

"You had offers.'' When her brows lifted, he shrugged. "You're representing my brother. I checked on you. Graduated top of your class at NYCC, passed the bar first shot, then turned down three very lucrative offers from three very prestigious firms to work for peanuts as a public defender. I had to figure either you were crazy or dedicated.''

She swallowed a little bubble of temper and nodded. "And you left the navy with a chestful of medals, including the Silver Star. Your file includes, along with a few reprimands for insubordination, a personal letter of gratitude from an admiral for your courage during a rescue at sea in a hurricane.'' Enjoying his squirm of embarrassment, she lifted her glass in toast. "I checked, too.''

"We were talking about you,'' he began.

"No. You were.'' Smiling, she cupped her chin on her hand. "So tell me, Muldoon, why did you turn down a shot at officer candidate school?''

"Didn't want to be a damn officer,'' he muttered. Rising, he grabbed her hand and hauled her to her feet. "Let's dance.''

She chuckled as he dragged her onto the crowded dance floor. "You're blushing.''

"I am not. And shut up.''

Rachel tucked her tongue in her cheek. "It must be hell being a hero.''

"Here's the deal." Zack held her lightly by the arms on the edge of the dance floor. "You drop the stuff about medals and admirals, and I won't mention that you were class valedictorian."

She thought it over. "Fair enough. But I think—"

He pulled her into his arms. "Stop thinking."

It did the trick, all right. The moment she found herself pressed hard against him, her mind clicked off. She could still hear the music, the low, seductive alto sax, the pulse of the bass, the slow rhythms of the piano notes, but rational thought vanished.

They weren't dancing. Rachel was certain no one would call this locked-hard, swaying embrace a dance. But it would be foolish to try to pull away when there was so little room. Breathing wasn't all that important, after all. Not when you could feel your own heart slamming against your ribs.

She hadn't intended to wind her arms quite so firmly around his neck, but now that they were there, there seemed little point in moving them. Besides, if she skimmed her fingers up just a bit, they could trail through his hair so that she could discover how fascinating that silky contrast was compared to the rock-hard body molded to hers.

"You fit." He bent his head so that his mouth was against her ear. "I was a little too wound up to be sure the other night. But I thought you would."

The subtle movements of his lips against her skin had her shivering before she could prevent it. "What?"

"Fit," he said again, letting his hands follow those curvy lines down to her hips and back again.

"That's only because I'm standing on my toes."

"Honey, height doesn't have a thing to do with it."
He rubbed his cheek against her hair, filling himself
with the scent, the texture. "You feel right, you smell
right, you taste right."

Shaken, she turned her head before his mouth could
finish its journey down the side of her face. "I could
have you arrested for trying to seduce me in a public
place."

"That's all right. I know a good lawyer." He trailed
his fingers under the back of her soft wool sweater to
the heated skin beneath.

Her breath caught, then released unsteadily.
"They'll have us both arrested."

"I'll post bail." There was nothing but Rachel under the sweater, he was sure of it. His mouth went dry
as dust. "I want you alone." Biting off a groan, he
dipped his head to press his lips to her neck. "Do you
know what I'd do to you right now if I had you
alone?"

She shook her swimming head. "We should sit
down. We shouldn't do this."

"I want to touch you, every inch of you. And taste
you. I want to make you crazy."

He already was. If she didn't manage to slow things
down, her overcharged system was likely to explode.
"Two steps back," she said on a long breath, and took
just that. His hands remained at her waist, but at least
she could breathe again. At least she managed two
gulps of air before she looked into his eyes and the
breath backed up in her lungs again. "Too much, too
fast, Muldoon. I'm not a spontaneous type of person."

What she *was* was a volcano ready to erupt. He was damn sure going to be there when the ground started to shake. But he didn't intend to scare her off, either. "Hey, you want time. I can give you an hour. Two, if you really want me to suffer."

She shook her head, edging back to the table. "Let's just say I'll let you know if and when I'm ready to take this any further."

"She wants me to suffer," Zack said under his breath. When she didn't sit, he reached for his wallet. "I take it we're leaving."

"An early evening," she reminded him. And she wanted badly to get outside, where the air could cool her blood.

"A deal's a deal." He tossed bills onto the table. "Why don't we walk back? A little exercise might help us both sleep tonight."

A twenty-block hike, Rachel mused. It couldn't hurt.

"Cold?" he asked a short time later.

"No. It's nice." But he slipped an arm around her shoulders anyway. "I don't often get a chance to just walk. Mostly it's a dash from my place to the office, from the office to the courthouse."

"What do you do when you're not dashing?"

"Oh, I go to the movies, window-shop, visit the family. In fact, I was thinking it might be good for Nick to go with me one Sunday. Have some of Mama's home cooking, listen to one of Papa's stories, see how my brothers harass me."

"Just Nick?"

She slanted him a look. "I suppose we could make room for Nick's brother."

"It's been a long time since I—since either of us had a family meal. How about the cop? I can't see him piping us aboard."

"I'll handle Alex." Now that she'd suggested it, her mind began to turn quickly. "You know, Natasha and her family are due to visit in a couple of weeks. Things will be crowded and crazy. It might be the perfect opportunity to toss Nick into your not-so-average-family type of situation. I'll see what I can work out."

"I know I thanked you before, but I don't think I know how to tell you how much I appreciate what you're doing for him."

"The court—"

"That's bilge, Rachel." They reached the steps of her building, and he turned her to face him. "You're not just filing weekly reports or representing a client. You put yourself out for Nick right from the start."

"Okay, so I've got a weak spot for bad boys. Don't let it get around."

"No, what you've got is class, and a good heart." He liked the way she looked in the shadowy light, the vitality that pulsed from her like breath, the snap of energy and embarrassment in her eyes. "It's a tough combination to beat."

She shrugged under his hands. "Now you're going to make me blush, Muldoon, so let's not get sloppy. If things work out the way we want, you can buy me more flowers at the end of the two months. We'll call it square." He let her back up one step, but then held her firm. She was uneasy, but she wasn't surprised. "Listen, it's been nice, but..."

"I don't figure you're going to ask me in."

"No," she said definitely, remembering how her body had reacted to him in a crowded club. "I'm not."

"So I'll just have to take care of this out here."

"Zack..."

"You know I'm not going to let you go without kissing you, Rachel." To tease them both, he skimmed his lips over her jaw. "Especially when I only have to touch you to know all the want's not on my side."

"This is never going to work," she murmured, but her arms were already sliding around him.

"Sure it will. We just put our lips together, and what happens happens."

This time she knew what to expect, and braced. It made no difference at all. The same heat, the same rush, the same power. The same reckless, unrelenting need. Had she said it was too much? No, it wasn't enough. She was afraid she could never get enough. How could she have lived her entire life without knowing what it was to be truly needy?

"I'm not getting involved this way," she murmured against his mouth. "Not with you. Not with anyone."

"Okay. Fine." Ruthlessly, he dragged her head back and plundered. A flash fire erupted between them until he felt singed down to the bone. He all but whimpered when she nipped impatiently at his lower lip. Images began to cartwheel in his head—him scooping her up and carrying her inside, falling with her into a big, soft bed. Making love with her on some white, deserted beach, with the sun beating down on her naked, golden skin. Waves pounding against the shore as she cried out his name.

"Hey, buddy."

The voice behind him was nothing more than an irritating buzzing in his head. Zack would cheerfully have ignored it, but he felt the slight prick of a knife at his back. Keeping Rachel behind him, he turned and looked into the pale, sooty-eyed face of the mugger.

"How about I let you keep the babe, and you hand over your wallet? Hers, too." The mugger turned the knife so that the backwash of the streetlight caught the steel. "And let's make it fast."

Blocking Rachel with his body, Zack reached in his back pocket. He could hear Rachel's unsteady breathing as she unzipped her bag. It wasn't impulse, but instinct. The moment the mugger's eyes shifted, Zack lunged.

With a scream in her throat and the Mace in her hand, Rachel watched them struggle. She saw the knife flash, heard the awful crunch of fist against bone before the blade clattered to the sidewalk. Then the mugger was racing off into the dark, and she and Zack were as alone as they'd been seconds before.

He turned back to her. She noted that he wasn't even breathing hard, and that the gleam in his eyes had only sharpened. "Where were we?"

"You idiot." The words were little more than a whisper as she fought to get them out over the lump of fear in her throat. "Don't you know any better than to jump someone holding a knife? He could have killed you."

"I didn't feel like losing my wallet." He glanced down at the can in her hand. "What's that?"

"Mace." Disgusted by the fact she hadn't even popped off the safety top, she dropped it back in her purse. "I'd have given him a faceful if you hadn't gotten in the way."

"Next time I'll step aside and let you handle it." He frowned down at the trickle of blood on his wrist and swore without much heat. "I guess he nicked me."

She went pale as water. "You're bleeding."

"I thought it was his." Annoyed more than hurt, he poked a finger through the rip in the arm of his sweater. "I got this on Corfu, my last time through. Damn it." Eyes narrowed, he stared down the street, wondering if he had a chance of catching up with the mugger and taking the price of the sweater, if not its sentimental value, out of his hide.

"Let me see." Her fingers trembled as she pushed the sleeve up to examine the long, shallow slash. "Idiot!" she said again, and began to fumble in her purse for her keys. "You'll have to come inside and let me fix it. I can't believe you did something so stupid."

"It was the principle," he began, but she cut him off with a stream of Ukrainian as she stabbed her key at the lock.

"English," he said, pressing a hand to his stomach as it began to knot. "Use English. You don't know what it does to me when you talk in Russian."

"It's not Russian." Snatching his good arm, she pulled him inside. "You were just showing off, that's all. Oh, it's just like a man." Still pulling him, she stalked into the elevator.

"Sorry." He was fighting off a grin, trying to look humble. "I don't know what got into me." He certainly wasn't going to admit he'd had worse scratches shaving.

"Testosterone," she said between her teeth. "You can't help it." She kept her hand on him until she'd gotten them inside her apartment. "Sit," she ordered, and dashed into the bathroom.

He sat, making himself at home by propping his feet on her coffee table. "Maybe I should have a brandy," he called out. "In case I'm going into shock."

She hurried back out with bandages and a small bowl of soapy water. "Do you feel sick?" Scared all over again, she pressed a hand to his brow. "Are you dizzy?"

"Let's see." Always willing to take advantage of an opportunity, he grabbed a fistful of her hair and pulled her mouth to his. "Yeah," he said when he let her go. "You could say I'm feeling a little lightheaded."

"Fool." She slapped his hand aside, then sat down to clean the wound. "This could have been serious."

"It was serious," he told her. "I hate having someone poke me in the back with a knife when I'm kissing a woman. Honey, if you don't stop shaking, I'm going to have to get *you* a brandy."

"I'm not shaking—or if I am, it's just because I'm mad." She tossed her hair back and glared at him. "Don't you ever do that again."

"Aye, aye, sir."

To pay him back for the smirk, she dumped iodine over the wound. When he swore, it was her turn to smile. "Baby," she said accusingly, but then took pity on him and blew the heat away. "Now hold still while I put a bandage on it."

He watched her work. It was very pleasant to feel her fingers on his skin. It seemed only natural that he should lean over to nibble at her ear.

Fire streaked straight up her spine. "Don't." Shifting out of reach, she pulled his sleeve down over the fresh bandage. "We're not going to pick things up now. Not here." Because if they did, she knew there would be no backing off.

"I want you, Rachel." He caught her hand in his before she could stand. "I want to make love with you."

"I know what you want. I have to know what I want."

"Before we were interrupted downstairs, I think that was pretty clear."

"To you, maybe." After a deep breath, she pulled her hand free and stood. "I told you, I don't do things spontaneously. And I certainly don't take a lover on impulse. If I act on the attraction I feel for you, I'll do so with a clear head."

"I don't think I've had a clear head since I laid eyes on you." He stood, as well, but because it suddenly seemed important to both of them he kept his distance. "I realize how the saying goes about guys like me and women in every port. That's not reality—not my reality, anyway. I'm not going to tell you I spent every liberty curled up with a good book, but..."

"It's not my business."

"I'm beginning to think it is, or could be." The look in his eyes kept her from arguing. "I've been on land for two years, and there hasn't been anybody important." He couldn't believe what he was saying, what he felt compelled to say, but the words just tumbled out. "I'll be damned if there's ever been anyone like you in my life."

"I have priorities…" she began. The words sounded weak to her. "And I don't know if I want this kind of complication right now. We have Nick to think about, as well, and I'd rather we just take it slow."

"Take it slow," he repeated. "I can't give you any promises on that. I *can* promise that the first chance I get, when it's just you and me, I'm going to do whatever it takes to shake up those priorities of yours."

She jammed nervous hands in her pockets. "I appreciate the warning, Muldoon. And here's one for you. I don't shake easily."

"Good." His grin flashed before he walked to the door. "Winning's no fun if it's easy. Thanks for the first aid, Counselor. Lock your door." He shut it quietly behind him and decided to walk home.

At this rate, he was never going to get any sleep.

Chapter Five

She wasn't avoiding him. Exactly. She was busy, that was all. Her caseload didn't allow time for her to drop by Zack's bar night after night and chat with the regulars. It wasn't as if she were neglecting her duty. She had slipped in a time or two to talk with Nick in the kitchen. If she'd managed to get in and out without running into Zack, it was merely coincidence.

And a healthy survival instinct.

If she let her answering machine screen her calls at home, it was simply because she didn't want to be disturbed unnecessarily.

Besides, he hadn't called. The jerk.

At least she was making some progress where Nick was concerned. He had called her, twice. Once at her office, and once at home. She found his suggestion that they catch a movie together a hopeful sign. After all, if he spent an evening with her, he wouldn't be hanging out with the Cobras, looking for trouble.

After ninety minutes of car chases, gunplay and the assorted mayhem of the action-adventure he'd chosen, they settled down in a brightly lit pizzeria.

"Okay, Nick, so tell me how it's going." His answer was a shrug, but Rachel gave his arm a squeeze and pressed. "Come on, you've had two weeks to get used to things. How are you feeling about it?"

"It could be worse." He pulled out a cigarette. "It's not so bad having a little change in my pocket, and I guess Rio's not so bad. It's not like he's on my case all the time."

"But Zack is?"

Nick blew out a stream of smoke. He liked to watch her through the haze. It made her look more mysterious, more exotic. "Maybe he's laid off a little. But it's like tonight. I got the night off, right? But he wants to know where I'm going, who I'm going with, when I'll be back. That kind of sh—" He caught himself. "That kind of stuff. I mean, hey, I'm going to be twenty in a couple of months. I don't need a keeper."

"He's a pushy guy," Rachel said, trying to strike a balance between sympathy and sternness. "But he's not only responsible for you in the eyes of the law—he cares about you." Because his answering snort seemed more automatic than sincere, she smiled. "His style's a little rough, but I'd have to say his intentions are good."

"He's going to have to give me some room."

"You're going to have to earn it." She squeezed his hand to take the sting out of her words. "What did you tell him about tonight?"

"I said I had a date, and he should butt out." Nick grinned, pleased when he saw the answering humor in Rachel's eyes. He'd have been very disappointed if he'd realized she was amused at the term *date*. "It's like he's got his life and I got mine. You know what I'm saying?"

"Yes." She drew a deep appreciative breath as their pizza arrived. "And what do you want to do with your life, Nick?"

"I figure I'll take what comes."

"No ambitions?" She took the first bite, watching him. "No dreams?"

Something flickered in his eyes before he lowered them. "I don't want to be serving drinks for a living, that's for sure. Zack can have it." After crushing out his cigarette, he applied himself to the pizza. "And no way I'm going into the damn navy, either. He swung that one by me the other day, and I shot it down big-time."

"Well, you seem to know what you don't want. That's a step."

He reached out to toy with the little silver ring on her finger. "Did you always want to be a lawyer?"

"Pretty much. For a while I wanted to be a ballerina, like my sister. That's when I was five. It only took about three lessons for me to figure out it wasn't all tutus and toe shoes. Then I thought I might be a carpenter, like the men in my family, so I asked for a tool set for my birthday. I think I was eight. I managed to build a pretty fair book rack before I retired." She smiled, and his heart rate accelerated. "It took me a while to come to the conclusion that I couldn't be what Natasha was, or Papa or Mama or anyone else.

I had to find my own way.'' She said it casually, hoping the concept would take root.

"So you went to law school."

"Mmm…" Her eyes brightened as she studied him. "Can you keep a secret?"

"Sure."

"Perry Mason." Laughing at herself, she scooped up another slice. "I was fascinated by those old reruns. You know, how there would always be this murder, and Perry would take the case when his client looked doomed. Lieutenant Tragg would have all this evidence, and Perry would have Della and Paul Drake out looking for clues to prove his client's innocence. Then they'd go to court. Lots of objections, and 'Your Honor, as usual the counsel for the defense is turning this proceeding into a circus.' It would look bad for Perry. He'd be up against that smug-faced DA."

"Hamilton Berger," Nick said, grinning.

"Right. Perry would play it real close to the vest, dropping little hints to Della, but never spilling the whole thing. You just knew he had all the answers, but he would string it out. Then, always at the eleventh hour, he'd get the real murderer up on the witness stand, and he'd just hammer the truth out of him, until the poor slob would crumble like a cookie and confess all."

"Then he'd explain how he'd figured it all out in the epilogue," Nick finished for her. "And you wanted to be Perry Mason."

"You bet," Rachel agreed over a bite of pizza. "By the time I realized it wasn't that black-and-white, and it certainly wasn't that tidy, I was hooked."

"Ray Charles," Nick said, half to himself.

"What?"

"It just made me think how listening to Ray Charles made me want to play the piano."

Rachel rested her chin on her folded hands and tried to ease the door open a little farther. "Do you play?"

"Not really. I used to think it would be pretty cool. Sometimes I'd hang around this music store and fiddle around until they kicked me out." The twinge of embarrassment made him brush the rest aside. "I got over it."

But once she had a purpose, Rachel wasn't easily shaken. "I always wished I'd learned. Tash got my mother a piano a few months ago—when we found out she'd always wanted to play. All those years we were growing up, she never mentioned it. All those years..." Her words trailed off, and then she shook herself back to the matter at hand. "My sister married a musician. Spencer Kimball."

"Kimball?" Nick's eyes widened before he could prevent it. "The composer?"

"You know his work?"

"Yeah." He struggled to keep it cool. A guy couldn't admit he listened to longhair music—unless it was heavy metal. "Some."

Delighted with his reaction, Rachel continued, just as casually. "At one of our visits down to see Tash and her family, we caught Mama at the piano. She got all flustered and kept saying how she was too old to learn, and how foolish it was. But then Spence sat down with her to show her a few chords, and you could see, you could just see, how much she wanted to learn. So on Mother's Day, we worked out this big, elaborate plan to get her out of the house for a few hours. Anyway, when she came back, the piano was in the living room. She cried." Rachel blinked the mist out of her own eyes and sighed. "She takes lessons twice a week now, and she's practicing for her first recital."

"That's cool," Nick murmured, obscurely touched.

"Yeah, it's pretty cool." She smiled at him. "I guess it proves it's never too late to try." When she offered a hand, she wanted him to take it as a gesture of friendship and support. "What do you say we walk off some of this pizza?"

"Yeah." His fingers closed around hers, and Nicholas LeBeck was in heaven.

He was content to listen to her talk, to have her laugh shiver over him. Even the shadows of the girls who had weaved in and out of his life faded away. They were nothing compared to the woman who walked beside him, slim and soft and fragrant.

She listened when he talked. And she was interested in what he had to say. When she smiled up at him, those exotic eyes flashing with humor, his stomach tied itself into slippery knots.

He could have walked with her for hours.

"This is it."

Nick pulled up short, standing in almost the exact spot his brother had a few nights before. As his gaze skimmed over the building at her back, he imagined what it would be like if she asked him in. They'd have coffee, and she'd slip off her shoes and curl those long legs up as they talked.

He'd be careful with her, even gentle. Once his nerves settled.

"I'm glad we could do this," she was saying, already taking out her keys. "I hope if you're feeling restless again, or just need to talk to someone, you'll call me. When I file my report with Judge Beckett tomorrow, I think she'll be pleased with the way things are working out."

"Are you?" His eyes locked on hers as he lifted a hand to her hair. "Pleased with the way things are working out?"

"Sure." A little alarm shrilled in Rachel's head, but she dismissed it as absurd. "I think you've taken a step in the right direction."

"Me too."

The alarm continued to beep as she backed up. "We'll have to do this again soon, but I've got to get in now. I have an early meeting."

"Okay. I'll call you."

She blinked as his hand slipped around to cup her neck. "Ah, Nick..."

His mouth closed over hers, very warm, very firm. Her eyes stayed open, registering shock, as her hand flew up to press against his shoulder. His fingers tensed against her neck, and she had the impression of a very lean, very hard body before she managed to pull away.

"Nick," she said again, groping.

"It's okay." He smiled, tucked her hair behind her ear in a gesture that reminded her vividly of his brother. "I'll be in touch."

He strolled away. No...good Lord, he was swaggering, Rachel thought as she stared after him. With her mind whirling, she let herself in. "Oh, boy," she sighed as she paced the elevator.

What now? What now? How could she have been so stupid? Cursing herself, she stomped off the elevator and toward her apartment. This was great, just great. Here she'd been trying to make friends with Nick, and all the while he'd been thinking...

She didn't want to think about what he'd been thinking.

Without taking off her jacket, she paced the apartment. There had to be a reasonable, diplomatic way to handle this, she told herself. He was only nineteen, he just had a crush, she was overreacting.

Then she remembered those limber fingers on the back of her neck, the firm press of those lips, the smooth and practiced way he'd drawn her against him.

Wrong, Rachel thought, and closed her eyes. She wasn't dealing with a child's puppy love, but with a full-grown man's desire.

Dropping down onto the arm of the couch, she dragged her hands through her hair. She should have seen it coming, she told herself. She should have stopped it before it started. She should have done a lot of things.

After twenty minutes of kicking herself, she snatched up the phone. She might be hip-deep in quicksand, but she wasn't going to sink alone.

"Lower the Boom."

"Let me talk to Muldoon," Rachel snapped, scowling at the sound of laughter and bar chatter that hummed through the receiver. "It's Rachel Stanislaski."

"You got it. Hey, Zack, phone for you. It's the babe."

Babe? Rachel thought, narrowing her eyes. "Babe?" she repeated out loud the moment Zack had answered.

"Hey, sugar, I'm not responsible for the opinions of my bartenders." He took a swallow of mineral water. "So you finally realized you couldn't keep away from me."

"Stuff it, Muldoon. We need to talk. Tonight."

He stopped grinning and shifted the phone. "Is there a problem?"

"Damn right."

"Nick breezed through a couple of minutes ago. He seemed fine when he headed upstairs."

"He's upstairs?" she said, calculating. "Just make sure he stays up there. I'm coming right over." She hung up before he could ask any questions.

It wasn't exactly the way he'd planned it, Zack thought as he mixed a couple of stingers. His strategy had been to lie back for a few days, let Rachel simmer. Until she came to a boil—and came looking for him.

She hadn't sounded lonely or aroused or vulnerable over the phone. She'd sounded mad as a hornet.

He cast his eyes up at the ceiling, picturing the apartment overhead, as he automatically added a twist to a glass of club soda. Obviously it had to do with Nick. Where the hell had the boy been all evening? he wondered.

What kind of trouble had he gotten himself into this time? With half an ear, Zack took an order for two drafts, a margarita on the rocks and a coffee, black. Damned if he'd thought the boy was in trouble, Zack reflected. Nick had looked relaxed, calm, even approachable, when he'd checked in. Zack remembered thinking that the date had been a rousing success. And he'd hoped to be able to ease the girl's name out of his brother—along with a bit more salient information.

He didn't figure Nick needed a course in the birds and bees, but he hoped to drop a few hints about responsibility, protection and respect.

A steady girl, a steady job, a stable home. They all seemed to be coming together. So what the hell . . .

His thoughts broke off as he looked up. Rachel walked in, cheeks flushed from the chilly evening, eyes snapping. As she crossed the room, she peeled off her jacket to reveal one of those soft sweaters she often wore. This one was the color of a good burgundy, with a wide cowl neck that draped softly over the swell of her breasts. It rode her hips, and under it she wore snug black leggings that showed off those first-class legs.

Zack checked to make sure his tongue wasn't hanging out.

She stopped at the bar only long enough to glare at him. "In your office." Without waiting for a response, she strode off.

"Well, well . . ." Lola watched Rachel swing Zack's office door open, then shut it behind her with a loud click. "Looks like the lady's got something on her mind."

"Yeah." Zack set the last glass on Lola's tray. All he could think was, there was definitely a fire in the hole. "If Nick comes back down, tell him I'm . . . tied up."

"You're the boss."

"Right." And he intended to remain the boss. He swung through the bar and, taking one bracing breath, marched into his office.

Rachel had tossed her jacket and purse aside, and was pacing. When the door opened, she stopped, swung her hair back and leveled a killing gaze at him.

"Don't you ever talk to him?" she demanded. "Aren't you making any effort to find out what's going on in his head? What kind of a guardian are you, anyway?"

"What the hell is this?" He threw up his hands in disgust. "I don't see or hear from you in days, then you come stalking in here just so you can yell at me. Just simmer down, Counselor, and remember I'm not some felon on the witness stand."

"Don't tell me to simmer down," she tossed back. It felt good, really good, to assuage her guilt and frustration with a pitched battle. "I'm the one who's going to have to deal with him. And if you were any kind of a brother, you would have known. You could have warned me."

Because his confidence as a brother was still at low tide, he hissed out an oath. Rachel echoed it as he shoved her into a chair. "Just sit down and take it from the top. I assume we're talking about Nick."

"Of course we're talking about Nick." She popped up again, and was pushed right back down. "I don't have anything else to discuss with you."

"We'll bypass that for now. Just what is it I should have known and warned you about?"

"That he'd...he'd..." She blew out a breath, struggling for the proper phrase. "That he'd started to think of me as a woman."

"How the hell is he supposed to think of you? As a tuna?"

"I mean as a *woman*," she said between her teeth. "Do I have to spell it out?"

His brows shot up, then settled again as he reached for a cigarette. "Don't be stupid, Rachel. He's nineteen. I'm not saying he's blind and wouldn't appreciate the way you look. But he's got a girl. He was out with her tonight."

"You idiot." She sprang up again, and this time she thumped a fist on his chest. "He was out with *me* tonight."

"Out with you?" With a frown, Zack studied her. "What for?"

"We went to the movies, had a pizza. I wanted to get him to talk a little—informally—so when he called I said sure."

"One step at a time. Nick called you and asked you out on a date."

"It wasn't a date. I didn't think it was a damn date." Since she didn't see anything handy to kick other than Zack's shin, she stalked a circle around his office again. "It seemed to me if we could develop a relationship— A friendship," she corrected hastily. "It would make things easier all around."

Considering, Zack took a drag of his cigarette. "Sounds reasonable. So you took in a flick and had a pizza. What's the problem? Did he get into a fight, give you a hard time?" He stopped, alarmed. "You didn't run in to any of the Cobras?"

"No, no, no..." Incensed, she whirled around the room. "Aren't you listening to me? I said he was thinking about me as a woman...as a date. As a... Oh, boy." She let out a long breath. "He kissed me."

Zack's eyes turned into dark, dangerous slits. "Define *kiss*."

"You know damn well what a kiss is. You smack your lips up against somebody's." She spun away, then back. "I should have seen it coming, but I didn't. Then, before I realized what he was thinking, wham!"

"Wham," Zack repeated, trying to stay calm. He took his own turn around the room, bumping his shoulders against hers. "Okay, listen, I think you're making a big deal out of nothing. He kissed you good-night. It's a gesture. He's just a kid."

"No," Rachel said, and her tone had Zack turning back to her. "He's not."

Temper was clawing to gain freedom. As a result, Zack's voice was deadly calm. "Did he try to—"

"No." Recognizing the signs, she cut him off. "Of course he didn't. He just kissed me. But it was the way... Listen, Zack, I know the difference between a casual kiss good-night between friends and—and, well, a move. And I can tell you Nick has a very smooth move."

"Glad to hear it," Zack said between his teeth.

Suddenly drained, she dropped down onto the corner of his desk. "I don't know what to do."

"I'll straighten him out."

"How?"

"I don't know how," he shot back, crushing out his cigarette. "I'll be damned if I'm going to be competing with my kid brother."

The muttered aside had her narrowing her eyes. "I'm not a trophy, Muldoon."

"I didn't mean—" With a shake of his head, he leaned on the desk beside her. "Look, this throws me off course, okay? I figured Nick was out making time with some pretty little teenager whose daddy would want her home by midnight, and now I find out he's coming on to you. If he wasn't my brother, I'd go knock him around a little."

"Typical," she muttered.

He ignored that and tried to think. "It's probably normal for him to develop—or think he's developed—feelings for you. Don't you think?"

"Maybe." She tilted her head to slant Zack a look. "I don't want to hurt him."

"Me either. You could back off, stay unavailable—the way you've tried to be with me."

"I've been busy." All dignity, she lifted her chin. "And we're not talking about you. In any case, I considered that, but I'm supposed to be his co-guardian. I can't do that long-distance. Besides, he talked to me tonight. He really talked, and relaxed, and showed me a little of what's underneath all that defiance. If I cut him off now, just when he's beginning to open up and trust me, I don't know what damage I might do."

"You can't string him along, Rachel."

"I know that." She wanted to lay her head on Zack's shoulder, just for a minute. She looked down at her hands instead. "I need to find a way to let him know I want to be his friend—just his friend—without crushing his ego."

Zack took her hand, and when she didn't pull it away he twined his fingers in hers. "I'll talk to him. Calmly," he added when Rachel frowned at him.

"Actually, I wanted to dump the whole business in your lap, but the more I think about it, the more I'm sure he'd only resent it coming from you. How can you tell him I'm not interested without letting him know we discussed his feelings behind his back?" She shut her eyes. "And I'm not feeling very good about that, either."

"You had to tell me."

"Yeah, I think I did, just like I think I'm going to have to figure out what to do."

He ran his thumb over her knuckles. "We're in this together, remember?"

"How can I forget? But you and Nick are just getting your balance. This is bound to tilt the scales, Zack. I think it's best if I try to handle it." A smile played around the corners of her mouth. "I guess I should apologize for coming here and jumping on you."

"At least it got you here. We'll handle it." He brought her hand to his lips, enjoying the way her eyes darkened and became cautious. "You let him down easy, and I'll let him take it out on me. After all, I can't blame the kid for trying, when I'm doing the same myself."

"One has nothing to do with the other." She pushed away from the desk, but he continued to hold her hand.

"I'm glad to hear it. Feeling better?"

Her lips quirked. "Fighting always makes me feel better."

"Then, sugar, by the time we're through with each other, you should be feeling like a million bucks. I don't suppose you'd like to hang around for a couple of hours until I can close the bar."

"No." Her heart picked up a beat at the thought. A dark, empty bar, blues on the juke, the world locked outside. "No, I have to go."

"I'm shorthanded tonight, or I'd see you home. I'll put you in a cab."

"I can put myself in a cab."

"Okay. In a minute." He caught her by the hips, lifted her, then set her on the desk. "I've missed you," he murmured, nuzzling her neck.

Without thinking—he certainly had a way of making her stop thinking—she tilted her head to give him more access to her skin. "I've been busy."

"I don't doubt you've been busy." He moved up to nip at her earlobe. "But you've been stubborn. I like that about you, Rachel. Right now I can't think of a damn thing I don't like about you."

This was a mistake. Any minute she'd remember why it was a mistake. She was sure of it. "You just want to talk me into bed."

His lips curved before they came down on hers. "Oh, yeah..." He fisted his hands in her hair, and a deep sound of pleasure came from his throat when she arched against him. "How'm I doing?"

"You're making things very difficult for me."

"Good. That's good." He was very close to pressing her back on the desk and doing all the things he'd fantasized about during those long, dark nights he'd lain alone in bed, thinking of her. And she sighed. The soft, broken sound of it seemed to rip something inside his gut. Grinding out an oath, he buried his face in her hair. "I sure pick my spots," he muttered. "On the sidewalk with a mugger, in my office with a barful of customers outside the door. Every time I'm around you I start acting like a kid in the back seat of a parked car.''

She had to concentrate just to breathe. As he continued to hold her, just hold her, she found herself stroking his hair, counting his heartbeats, warming toward him in a way that was entirely different from the flash heat of a moment before.

She'd been right about the quicksand, she realized. And she'd been right about not sinking alone. ''We're not kids,'' she murmured.

''No, we're not.'' Not quite sure he could trust himself, he drew back, taking both her hands in his. ''I know it's moving fast, and I know it's complicated, but I want you. There's no getting around it.''

''I knew this would happen if I came here tonight. I came anyway.'' Muddled, she shook her head. ''I don't know what that says about me, or about us. I do know it's not smart, and I'm usually smart. The best thing for me to do is walk out the door and go home.''

He tugged on her hands, bringing her off the desk and close to him again. ''What are you going to do?''

She wavered, caught on the thin edge between temptation and common sense. Images of what could be swam giddily through her head and left her throat dry. Repercussions . . . she couldn't quite see them clearly, but she knew they existed. And she was afraid they would be severe indeed.

''I'm going to walk out the door and go home.'' She let out an unsteady breath when he said nothing. ''For now.''

She grabbed up her jacket, her purse. When she reached the door, his hand closed over hers on the knob. A quick thrill of panicked excitement raced through her at the thought that he would simply turn the lock.

She wouldn't permit it. Of course she wouldn't permit it.

Would she?

"Sunday" was all he said.

Her scattered thoughts scrambled to make sense of the word. "Sunday?"

"I can shift things around and take the day off. Spend it with me."

Relief. Confusion. Pleasure. She had no idea which emotion was uppermost. "You want to spend Sunday with me."

"Yeah. You know, take in a couple of museums, maybe an art gallery, a walk in the park, have a fancy lunch somewhere. I figure most of the time we've spent together so far's been after dark."

Odd...that hadn't occurred to her before. "I guess it has."

"Why don't we try a Sunday afternoon?"

"I..." She couldn't think of a single reason why not. "All right. Why don't you come by around eleven?"

"I'll be there."

She turned the knob, then glanced back at him. "Museums?" she said on a laugh. "Is this on the level, Muldoon?"

"I happen to appreciate art," he told her, leaning forward to touch his lips to hers in a quiet kiss that rocked her back on her heels. "And beauty."

She slipped out quickly. As she walked up to the

corner to hail a cab, it occurred to her she hadn't yet decided how best to handle Nick. And she sure as hell hadn't figured out how to handle Nick's big brother.

Chapter Six

Rachel was cursing when her buzzer sounded promptly at eleven o'clock Sunday morning. Securing an earring, she pressed the intercom. "Muldoon?"

"You sound out of breath, sugar. Should I take that as a compliment?"

"Come on up," she said shortly. "And don't call me sugar."

After snapping off the intercom, she flipped off her three security locks, then gave herself one last look in the mirror. She'd forgotten her second earring. Grumbling, she went on a quick search until she found it lying on the kitchen counter beside her empty coffee cup.

It was her day off, damn it. And she resented having it interrupted for work. Not because she'd been looking forward to spending it with Zack. Particularly. It was just that it had been a long time since she'd had a day to wander through museums and galleries, and— She broke off her silent complaining at the knock on the door.

"Come in, it's open."

"Anxious?" Zack commented as he walked in. Then he lifted a brow and took one long look. She was standing in the center of the room, slim and lovely in a bronze-toned suede jacket and short skirt set off by a slightly mannish silk blouse in a flashy blue. She was barefoot, and he found his mouth watering as he watched her perform the feminine and oddly intimate task of securing a shiny gold knot to her ear. "You look nice."

"Thanks. You, too." No, what he looked was sexy, she thought, damn sexy, in snug black jeans, a midnight-blue sweater, and a bomber jacket in soft black leather. But *nice* would have to do. "Listen, Zack, I tried to catch you before you left the bar. I'm sorry I missed you."

"Is there a problem?" He watched as she wiggled one foot into a bronze-colored pump. By the time she'd wiggled into the second, his palms were sweaty and he'd missed what she'd said. "Sorry, what?"

"I said my boss called, about a half hour ago. I've got an attempted murder I have to deal with."

That cut his fantasy off as quickly as a faceful of ice water. "A what?"

"Attempted murder. Alexi's precinct. I can probably plead down to assault with a deadly weapon, but I have to see him today so I can meet with the DA in the morning." She spread her hands. "I'm really sorry I didn't catch you before you came all the way over."

"No problem. I'll go with you."

"With me?" She liked the idea, a little too much. "You don't want to spoil your day off spending it at a police station."

"I'm taking the day off to be with you," he reminded her, and picked up her coat where she'd tossed it over the back of the couch. "Besides, it won't take all day, will it?"

"No, probably no more than an hour, but—"

"So let's get started." He walked to her, then turned her around so that he could slip the coat slowly on one arm, then the other. Lowering his head, he sniffed at her neck. "Did you spray that stuff on for the felon, or for me?"

She shivered once before cautiously stepping away. "For me." Picking up her briefcase, she held it between them like a shield. "I have to go by the office first. We already have a file on the guy. He's been around."

"Okay." He tugged the briefcase away, took her hand. "Let's go, Counselor."

Alex spotted his sister the moment she walked into the station. Since he wasn't any happier than she to be spending his Sunday morning at work, he immediately brightened. Giving Rachel a hard time always lifted his spirits.

Grinning, he strolled over, a greeting on his lips. When he spotted the man hovering around her, the humor in his eyes turned instantly to suspicion. "Rach."

Still clipping her visitor's badge to her lapel, she glanced up. "Alex. They got you, too, huh?"

"Looks like. Muldoon, isn't it?"

"That's right." Zack returned the steady stare and nodded. "Nice to see you again, Officer."

"Detective," Alex corrected. "I didn't hear anything about LeBeck being pulled in."

"I'm not here about Nick." Rachel recognized Alex's unfriendly, aggressive stance. He'd assumed it with every boy and man she'd dated since she'd turned fifteen. "I'm representing Victor Lomez."

"Now that's real slime." But Alex wasn't nearly as concerned about Rachel's client as he was with the reason the big Irishman was carrying her briefcase. "So, did you two run into each other outside?"

"No, Alexi." Rachel commandeered the coffee he was carrying. Though she knew it was worthless, she shot him a warning glance. "Zack and I had plans for the day."

"What kind of plans?"

"The kind that aren't any of your business." She kissed his cheek as an excuse to get close enough to his ear to whisper, "Knock it off." Leaning back, she smiled at Zack. "Grab a seat, Muldoon, and some of this horrible coffee. Like I said, this shouldn't take too long."

"I got all day," he told her as she walked off to a conference room. He turned back to Alex and said blandly, "So, you want to take me down to interrogation?"

Alex told himself he wasn't particularly amused, and gestured with a jerk of his head. "In here'll do." It pleased him to be behind his desk while Zack sat in the chair used to grill witnesses. "What's the story, Muldoon?"

Casually Zack took out a cigarette. He offered one to Alex and lit up when Alex shook his head. "You want to know what I'm doing with your sister." He blew out a stream of smoke, considering. "If you're any kind of detective, you should be able to figure that one out. She's beautiful, she's smart. She's a soft heart in a tough, sexy shell." Taking another drag, he watched Alex's eyes narrow. "Listen, you want it straight, or do you want me to tell you I'm just interested in her legal services?"

"Watch your step."

Because he understood the need to protect what he loved, Zack leaned forward. "Stanislaski, if you know Rachel, you know *she's* been watching my step. Nobody, but nobody, pushes her into something she doesn't want."

"You figure you got her pegged?"

"Are you kidding?" Zack's smile came quickly, and was friendly enough to make Alex's shoulders relax. "There isn't a man alive who really understands a woman. Especially a smart one." When he saw Alex's eyes shift over his shoulder, Zack glanced around. He saw a short, wiry, oily-skinned man being hauled toward the conference room by a uniformed cop. "Is that the one?"

"Yeah, that's Lomez."

Zack hissed smoke through his teeth and swore roundly. Alex could only agree.

At the conference table, Rachel looked up. Though she'd represented Lomez on his last count of assault, she was going over his file. "Well, Lomez, we meet again."

"You took your sweet time getting here." He dropped down in the seat and ignored the hovering cop. But he was sweating. Bungling the mugging meant he'd missed his connection. He hadn't had a fix in fourteen hours. "You bring me a smoke this time?"

"No. Thank you, Officer." Rachel waited until she was alone with her client, then folded her hands over his paperwork. "Well, you really pulled a prize this time out. The woman you attacked was sixty-three. I called the hospital this morning. You should be relieved to know they've bumped her condition up from critical to fair."

Lomez shrugged, his small black eyes gleaming at Rachel. He couldn't keep his hands still. He began to beat a tattoo on the table with his fingertips as he tapped his feet. His system was skidding to a much wilder rhythm. "Hey, if she'd handed over her purse like I told her, I wouldn't have had to get rough, you know?"

God, he sickened her, Rachel thought, fighting to remember she was a public servant. And Lomez, however revolting, was the public. "Knifing a senior citizen isn't going to win you the key to the city. It's sure as hell going to buy you a lock. Damn it, Lomez, she had twelve dollars."

His mouth was dry, and his skin was cold. "Then it wouldn't have cost her a lot to hand it over. You just get me out. That's your job." And the minute he was back on the street, he'd pressure one of the other Hombres to score for him. "I had to sit in that stinking cell all night."

"You're charged with attempted murder," Rachel said flatly.

Lomez tapped his damp hands against his thighs. Even his bones were screaming. "I didn't kill the old bitch."

Rachel wished she hadn't finished the coffee. At least she could have used it to wash some of the disgust out of her mouth. "You stuck a knife in her, three times. The officer responding pursued you as you fled the scene—with the knife and the victim's purse. They've got you cold, Lomez, and your priors aren't going to make the judge think leniency. Your repertoire includes assault, assault and battery, breaking and entering and two counts of possession."

"I don't need a list. I need bail."

"Odds are slim the DA's going to agree to bail, and if he does, it'll be well out of your range. Now I'm going to do what I can to get him to toss the attempted murder. You plead guilty to—"

"Guilty, my butt."

"It's going to be your butt," she said evenly. "You're not going to walk away from this one, Lomez. No matter how many rabbits I pull out of my hat, you're not going to do short time this turn around. Plead guilty to assault with a deadly weapon, it's likely I can swing the judge for seven to ten."

Sweat popped cold on his brow, on his lips. "The hell with that."

Because she was fast running out of patience, she slapped his file closed. "It won't get any sweeter. You cooperate, and I should be able to keep you from spending the next twenty years in a cage."

He screamed at her, then leaped across the table and struck before she had a chance to dodge. The back-handed blow knocked her out of her chair and onto the floor, where he fell on her. "You get me out!" He squeezed his hands on her throat, too wired even to feel her nails rake his wrist. "You bitch, you get me out or I'll kill you!"

At first she could only see his face, the sick rage in it. Then it faded as red dots swam in front of her eyes. Choking, she struck out, smashing the heel of her hand against the bridge of his nose. His blood splattered over her, but his hands tightened.

A roaring filled her ears, buzzing over the wild curses he shouted at her. The red dots faded to gray as she bucked under him.

Then her windpipe was free and she was sucking air down her burning throat. Someone was calling her name, desperately, and she was being lifted, held tight. She thought she smelled the scent of the sea before she fell limply into it.

Cool fingers on her face. Wonderful. Strong hands clasped hard over hers. Comforting. A sigh before waking. Agony.

Rachel blinked her eyes open. Two faces were looming over hers, equally grim, with eyes that held both rage and fear. Woozily she lifted a hand to Zack's cheek, then Alex's. "I'm all right." Her voice was husky, bruises already forming on her throat.

"Just lie still," Alex murmured in Ukrainian, stroking her head with a hand that still throbbed from where it had connected with Lomez's face. "Can you drink some water?"

She nodded. "I want to sit up." As she focused on the room, she realized she was lying on the faded couch in the captain's office. Murmuring her thanks to her brother, she sipped from the paper cup he held to her lips. "Lomez?"

"In a cage, where he belongs." Fighting off the tremors of reaction, Alex lowered his brow to hers. He continued to speak in Ukrainian, kissing her brow, her cheeks, then sitting back on his heels to hold her hand. "You just relax. An ambulance is on the way."

"I don't need an ambulance." Reading the argument in his eyes, she shook her head. "I don't." She glanced down to see that her blouse was gaping open. It was ruined, of course, she thought in disgust. That and her suede skirt were spotted with blood. "His blood, not mine," she pointed out.

"You broke his slimy low-life nose," Alex snapped.

"I'm glad my self-defense class wasn't wasted." When he began to swear, she caught his hand. "Alexi," she began, her voice low, intense. "Do you know what it is for me to accept that you risk your life every day, every night? Do you know I accept only because I love you so much?"

"Don't turn this around on me," he said furiously. "That bastard nearly killed you. He was so far gone it took three of us to drag him off."

She didn't want to think about that just yet. She couldn't. "I played it wrong."

"You—"

"I did," she insisted. "But the point is, we can't change what we are. I won't change, not even for you. Now cancel the ambulance and do something for me."

He called her a name, a rude one, in their native language. It made her smile. "I'm no more of a horse's ass than you. I need to contact my office and explain. I won't be able to represent Lomez under the circumstances."

"Damn right you won't." It was small satisfaction, but he could hope for little more. Gently he touched his fingers to the bruise on her cheekbone. "He's going down, Rachel. I'll make damn sure he goes down for this, if nothing else. There's nothing you or anyone else can do."

"That's for the courts to decide." She got shakily to her feet. "And you will not call Mama and Papa." When he said nothing, she lifted a brow. "If you do, I'll have to tell them about your last undercover assignment. The one where you went through the second-story window."

"Go home," he said, giving up. "Get some rest." He turned away from her to study Zack. His opinion of him had changed a bit, since Zack had been one of the three who'd hauled Lomez off Rachel. Alex had been a cop long enough to recognize murder in a man's eyes, and it had shone darkly in Zack's. He assumed, correctly, that Zack would have dealt with Lomez himself, regardless of cops, if he hadn't been so busy cradling Rachel in his arms. "You'll get her there." It wasn't a question.

"Count on it." He said nothing else as Alex left them.

Unsteady, and far from sure of herself, Rachel tried to smile. "Some date, huh?"

A muscle jumped in his jaw as he studied her spattered blouse. "Can you walk?"

"Of course I can walk." She hoped. The little seed of annoyance his terse question planted helped her get across the room. "Look, I'm sorry things got messed up this way. You don't have to—"

"Do me a favor," he said as he took her arm and led her through the squad room. "Just shut up."

She obliged him, though she was sorely tempted to tell him how foolish it was to indulge in a cab for the few blocks to her building. It was better if she didn't talk, she realized. Not only did it hurt, but she was also afraid her voice would begin to shake as much as her body wanted to.

She'd be alone in a few minutes, she reminded herself. Then she'd be able to indulge in a nice bout of trembling and weeping if she wanted to. But not in front of Zack. Not in front of anybody.

With a drunk's exaggerated care, she stepped out of the cab and onto the sidewalk. Mild shock, she deduced. It would pass. She'd make it pass.

"Thanks," she began. "I'm sorry..."

"I'm taking you up."

"Look, I've already ruined your morning. It isn't necessary to—" But he was already half carrying her to the door.

"Didn't I tell you to shut up?" He pulled open her briefcase to look for her keys himself. White-hot rage had his fingers fumbling. Didn't she know how pale she was? Couldn't she understand what it did to him inside to hear the way her voice rasped?

He pulled her through the door, into the elevator, and jabbed his finger on the button.

"I don't know what you're so mad about," she muttered, wincing a little as she swallowed. "You lost a couple of hours, sure, but do you know what I paid for this suit? And I've only worn it twice." Tears sprang to her eyes, and she blinked them back furiously as he dragged her down the hall to her apartment. "A PD's salary isn't exactly princely." She rubbed ice-cold hands together as he unlocked her door. "I had to eat yogurt for a month to afford it, even on sale. And I don't even like yogurt."

The first tear spilled out. She dashed it away as she walked inside. "Even if I could get it cleaned, I wouldn't be able to wear it after—" She broke off and made an enormous effort to pull herself back. She was babbling about a suit, for God's sake. Maybe she was losing her mind.

"Okay." She let out what she thought was a slow, careful breath. It hitched as it came out. "You got me home. I appreciate it. Now go away."

He merely tossed her briefcase aside, then tugged the coat from her shoulders. "Sit down, Rachel."

"I don't want to sit down." Another tear. It was too late to stop it. "What I want is to be alone." When her voice broke, she pressed her hands to her face. "Oh, God, leave me alone."

He picked her up, moving to the couch to hold her in his lap. Stroking her back through the tremors, feeling her tears hot and damp on his neck. He forced his hands to be gentle, even as the rage and fear worked inside him. As she curled up against him, he closed his eyes and murmured the useless words that always seemed to comfort.

She cried hard, he realized. But she didn't cry long. She trembled violently, but the trembling was soon controlled. She didn't try to push away. If she had, he wouldn't have allowed it. Perhaps he was comforting her. But holding her, knowing she was safe, and with him, brought him tremendous comfort.

"Damn it." When the worst was over, she let her head lie weakly on his shoulder. "I told you to go away."

"We had a deal, remember? You're spending the day with me." His hands tightened once, convulsively, before he managed to gentle them again. "You scared me, big-time."

"Me, too."

"And if I go away, I'm going to have to go back down there, find a way to get to that son of a bitch, and break him in half."

It was odd how a threat delivered so matter-of-factly could seem twice as deadly as a shout. "Then I guess you'd better hang around until the impulse fades. I'm really all right," she told him, but she left her head cuddled against his shoulder. "This was just reaction."

There was still an ice floe of fury in his gut. That was his reaction, and he'd deal with it later. "It may be his blood, Rachel, but they're your bruises."

Frowning, she touched fingers gingerly to her cheek. "How bad does it look?"

Despite himself, he chuckled. "Lord, I didn't know you were that vain."

She bristled, pulling back far enough to scowl at him. "It has nothing to do with vanity. I have a meeting in the morning, and I don't need all the questions."

He cupped her chin, tilted her head to the side. "Take it from someone who's had his share of bruises, sugar. You're going to get the questions. Now forget about tomorrow." He touched his lips, very gently, to the bruise, and made her heart stutter. "Have you got any tea bags? Any honey?"

"Probably. Why?"

"Since you won't go to the hospital, you'll have to put up with Muldoon first aid." He shifted her from his lap and propped her against the pillows. Their vivid colors only made her appear paler. "Stay."

Since the bout of weeping had tired her, she didn't argue. When Zack came out of the kitchen five minutes later, tea steaming in the cup in his hands, she was out like a light.

She awakened groggy, her throat on fire. The room was dim and utterly quiet, disorienting her. Pushing herself up on her elbows, she saw that the curtains had been drawn. The bright afghan her mother had crocheted years before had been tucked around her.

Groaning only a little, she tossed it aside and stood up. Steady, she thought with some satisfaction. You couldn't keep a Stanislaski down.

But this one needed about a gallon of water to ease the flames in her throat. Rubbing her eyes, she padded into the kitchen, then let out a shriek that seared her abused throat when she spotted Zack bending over the stove.

"What the hell are you doing? I thought you were gone."

"Nope." He stirred the contents of the pot on the stove before turning to study her. Her color was back, and the glazed look had faded from her eyes. It would take a great deal longer for the bruises to disappear. "I had Rio send over some soup. Do you think you can eat now?''

"I guess.'' She pressed a hand to her stomach. She was starving, but she wasn't sure how she was going to manage getting anything down her throbbing throat. "What time is it?''

"About three.''

She'd slept nearly two hours, she realized, and found the idea of her dozing on the couch while Zack puttered in the kitchen both embarrassing and touching. "You didn't have to hang around.''

"You know, your throat would feel better sooner if you didn't talk so much. Go in and sit down.''

Since the scent of the soup was making her mouth water, she obliged him. After tugging the curtains open, she sat at the little gateleg table by the window. With some disgust, she shrugged out of her stained jacket and tossed it aside. As soon as she'd indulged herself with some of Rio's soup, she would shower and change.

Obviously Zack had found his way around her kitchen, Rachel mused as he came in carrying bowls and mugs on a tray.

"Thanks.'' She saw his gaze light briefly on the jacket, heat, then flatten.

"I pawed through some of your records while you were out.'' It pleased him that he could speak casually when he wanted to break something. Someone. "Mind if I put one on?''

"No, go ahead.''

Watching the steam, she stirred her soup while he put an old B. B. King album on her stereo. "And they said we had nothing in common.''

Relieved that he wasn't going to bring the incident up, she smiled. "I stole it from Mikhail. He has very eclectic taste in music." Once Zack was seated across from her, she spooned up soup and swallowed gingerly. Sighed. It soothed her fevered throat the way a mother soothes a fretful child. "Wonderful. What's in it?"

"I never ask. Rio never tells."

With a murmur of acknowledgment, she continued to eat. "I'll have to figure out how to bribe him. My mother would love the recipe for this." She switched to tea. After the first sip, her eyes opened wide.

"You didn't have honey," Zack said mildly. "But you had brandy."

She took another, more cautious sip. "It ought to dull the nerve endings."

"That's the idea." Reaching across the table, he took her hand. "Feel any better?"

"Lots. I really am sorry you had your Sunday wrecked."

"Don't make me tell you to shut up again."

She only smiled. "I'm starting to think you're not such a bad guy, Muldoon."

"Maybe I should have brought you soup before."

"The soup helped." She spooned up some more. "But not making me feel like an idiot when I was crying all over you did the trick."

"You had pretty good cause. Being tough's not always the answer."

"It usually works." She sipped more of the brandy-laced tea. "I didn't want to let go in front of Alex. He worries enough." Her lips curved. "You know how it is to have a younger sibling who refuses to see things the way you do.''

"You mean so you'd like to rap their head against the wall? Yeah, I know.''

"Well, whether Alex likes to believe it or not, I can handle my own life. Nick will, too, when the time comes.''

"He's not like that creep today,'' Zack said softly. "He never could be.''

"Of course not.'' Concerned, she pushed her bowl aside. This time she took his hand. "You mustn't even think like that. Listen to me. For two years I've seen them come in and go out. Some are twisted beyond redemption, like Lomez. Others are desperate and confused, either battered by the streets or part of the streets. Working with them, it gets to the point that if you don't burn out or just scab over, you learn to recognize the nuances. Nick's been hurt, and his self-esteem is next to zero. He turned to a gang because he needed to be part of something, anything. Now he has you. No matter how much he might try to shake you loose, he wants you. He needs you.''

"Maybe. If he ever starts to trust me, he might be able to turn a corner.'' He hadn't realized how much it was weighing on him. "He won't talk to me about my father, about what it was like when I was gone.''

"He will, when he's ready.''

"The old man wasn't so bad, Rachel. He'd never have made father of the year, but—hell.'' He let out a breath in disgust. "He was a hard-nosed, hard-drinking Irish son of a bitch who should never have given up the sea. He ran our lives like we were green crewmen on a sinking ship. All shouts and bluster and the back of his hand. We never agreed on a damn thing.''

"Families often don't.''

"He never got over my mother. He was in the South Pacific when she died.''

Which meant Zack would have been alone. A child, alone. Her fingers tightened on his.

"He came back, mad as hell. He was going to make a man out of me. Then Nadine and Nick came along, and I was old enough to go my own way. You could say I abandoned ship. So he tried to make a man—his kind of man—out of Nick.''

"You're beating yourself up again over something you can't change. And couldn't have changed.''

"I guess I keep remembering how it was that first year I came back. The old man was so fragile. He couldn't remember things, kept wandering out and getting lost. Damn it, I knew Nick was running wild, but I didn't have my legs under me. Having to put the old man in a home, watching him die there, trying to keep the bar going. Nick got lost in the shuffle.''

"You found him again.''

He started to speak again, then sat back with a sigh. "Hell of a time to be dumping this on you.''

"It's all right. I want to help.''

"You've already helped. Do you want more soup?''

Subject closed, Rachel realized. She could press, or she could give him room. One favor deserved another, she decided, and smiled. "No, thanks. It really did the job.''

He wanted to say more, a whole lot more. He wanted to hold her again, and feel her head resting on his shoulder. He wanted to sit and watch her sleep on the couch again. And if he did any one of those things, he wouldn't make it to the door.

"I'll clear it up and get out of your hair. I imagine you'd like some time alone."

She frowned after him as he walked into the kitchen. She had wanted time alone, hadn't she? So why was she trying to think of ways to stall him, keep him from walking out the door.

"Hey, look." She pushed away from the table to wander in after him. He was already pouring the remaining soup in a container. "It's still early. We might be able to salvage some of the day."

"You need rest."

"I had rest." Feeling awkward, she ran water over the bowls he'd stacked in the sink. "We could probably make at least one museum, or catch a matinee. I don't want to think you spent your whole day off mopping up after me."

"Will you quit worrying about my day off?" Zack slapped the container on a shelf in the refrigerator. "I'm the boss, remember? I can take another."

"Fine." She slammed the water off. "See you around."

"Man, you've got a short fuse." Amused, he put his hands on her shoulders and rubbed. "Don't get yourself worked up, sugar. All in all, I had a very eventful day."

She closed her eyes, feeling those rough fingers through the silk of her blouse. "Any time, Muldoon."

He could smell her hair, and he had to fight the urge to bury his face in it. It wouldn't be possible to stop there. "You going to be all right alone? I could call the cop to come stay with you."

"No. I'm fine." Gripping the edge of the counter, she stared hard at the wall. "Thanks for the first aid."

"My pleasure." Damn it, he was stalling when he should be out the door. Away from her. "Maybe we can have an early dinner one night this week."

She pressed her lips together. The way his hands were rubbing up and down her arms made her want to whimper. "Sure. I'll check my schedule."

He turned her around. He couldn't be sure if she moved into his arms or if he'd pulled her there, but he was holding her. Her lips were parting for his. "I'll call you."

"Okay." Her eyes fluttered closed as the kiss deepened.

"Soon." He felt the breath backing up in his lungs as she molded against him.

"Um-hmm..." As his tongue danced over hers, she gave a quick sigh that caught in the middle.

He tore his mouth away to nibble along her jaw. "One more thing."

"Yes?"

"I'm not leaving."

"I know." Her arms curled around his neck as he lifted her. "It's just chemistry."

"Right." Struggling to remember her bruises, he rained soft kisses over her face.

"Nothing serious." She shuddered, nipping at his neck. "I can't afford to get involved. I have plans."

"Nothing serious," he agreed, blood pounding in his head, in his loins. He jerked open a door and found himself facing a closet. "Where's the damn bedroom?"

"What?" She focused, realized he'd carried her out of the kitchen. "This is it. The couch..." She nipped his ear. "It pulls out. I can..."

"Never mind," he managed, and settled for the rug.

Chapter Seven

He ripped her blouse. It wasn't only passion that made him grab and tear. He couldn't bear to see her wear it another moment, to see that vivid blue stained with spots of blood.

Yet the sound of it, of the silk rending beneath his fingers, and her gasp of shocked excitement, spread fire through his gut.

"The first time I saw you..." His breath was already short and fast when he tossed the mangled blouse aside. "From the first minute, I wanted this. Wanted you."

"I know." She reached for him, amazed at how deep and ripe a need could be. "Me, too. It's crazy," she said against his mouth. "Insane." Her skin trembled as he tugged the straps of her chemise from her shoulders to replace them with impatient lips. "Incredible."

Glorying in it, she arched against him when he took her breasts in those greedy, rough-palmed hands. Then his mouth—oh, his mouth, hot and seeking—closed over her to tug and suckle. *Hurry,* was all she could think, *hurry, hurry,* and her nails scraped heedlessly up his sides as she dragged his sweater over his head.

Flesh to flesh was what she wanted. Skin already hot, already damp. The feel of his lips against her thundering heart had her locking her fists in his hair, pressing him closer. She fretted for more. Even as the storm built to a crisis point inside her, she met, she ached, and she demanded.

Her fingers dug into his broad shoulders when he slid down, setting off hundreds of tiny eruptions by streaking hungry, openmouthed kisses down her torso. Then back, quickly back, to drown her in desire with his lips on hers.

He couldn't stop himself from taking. No matter that he had once imagined making slow, tortuously slow, love to her on some huge, soft bed. The desperation of what was overpowered any fantasy of what might have been.

She possessed him. Obsessed him. No mystical siren could have stolen his mind and soul more completely.

A button popped from her skirt as he fought to drag it down her hips. He thought he might go mad if he didn't rip aside all obstacles, if he didn't see her. All of her.

Half-crazed, he peeled off her stockings, and the delicate lace that had secured them. Somewhere

through the roaring in his brain he heard her throaty
cry when his fingers brushed against her thigh. Fighting to hold back, he knelt between her legs, filling
himself with the sight of her, slim and golden and naked, her hair tousled around her face, her eyes dark
and heavy.

She reared up, too desperate to wait even another
moment. Her mouth closed avidly over his, and her
fingers tore at the snap of his jeans.

"Let me," she said in a husky whisper.

"No." He slipped a hand behind her back to support her, and brought the other down to cover the
source of heat. "Let me."

The volcano he'd imagined erupted at the first
touch. Her body shuddered, quaked. And he watched,
impossibly aroused, as her head fell back. Not surrender. Even in his own delirium, he understood that
she was not surrendering. It was abandonment, the
pure, unleashed quest for pleasure. He gave her more,
and gave to himself, stroking that velvet fire, letting
his tongue slide over hers in a delicious, matching
rhythm.

How could she have known that desire could be
dark and deadly? Or that she, always so sure, always
so cautious, would throw reason to the winds for more
of the dangerous delights? No, not just more. All of
them, she thought dizzily. All of him. She would have
all. Locking her legs around his hips, she took him
into her.

She heard his gasp—the first one ended with a
groan. She saw his eyes, cobalt now, and fixed on hers
as he shifted to fill her. A sword to the hilt. Then he

moved, and she with him. Lost in the whirlwind, she heard nothing but the screaming of her own heart.

"The bigger they are," Rachel murmured some time later.

"Hmm?"

Smiling to herself, she lifted one of Zack's hands, let it go and watched it drop limply to the rug. "The harder they fall." She rolled over and propped her elbows on his chest so that she could study him. If she hadn't known better, she would have thought he was sleeping—or unconscious. His breathing had slowed—somewhat—but his eyes were still closed. It had been some time since he'd moved a single muscle.

"You know, Muldoon, you look like you went ten rounds with the champ."

His lips curved. It was about all he had the energy for. "You pack a hell of a punch, sugar."

As a matter of principle, she bit his shoulder. "Don't call me 'sugar.' But, since you mention it, you didn't do too badly yourself."

He opened one eye. "Too badly? I melted you down to a gooey puddle."

True enough, she admitted, but she wouldn't stroke his ego by agreeing. "I'll say that you have a certain unrefined style that is strangely appealing." She trailed a fingertip down his chest. "But the simple fact is, I had to carry you." That got his other eye open, she thought with satisfaction. "Not that I minded. I didn't have anything else pressing to do this afternoon."

"You carried me?"

"Metaphorically speaking."

His opinion of that was short and rude. "Want to take me on again? Champ?"

She fluttered her lashes. "Any time. Any place."

"Here and now." She was laughing as he rolled her over, but the laughter ended on a hiss of pain when he bumped her bruised cheek. "Klutz," she said as he jerked back and swore.

"I'm sorry."

"Come on, Zack." She smiled, wanting to lighten the concern in his eyes and bring back the laughter. "I was only kidding."

Ignoring that, he turned her head for a closer look at the mark on her cheek. "I should have put ice on that. He didn't break the skin, but it's..."

She could feel the tension hardening his shoulders. Instead of trying to stroke it away, she pinched him. "Listen, Buster, I come from tough stock. I got worse than that wrestling with my brothers."

"If he ever gets out—"

"Stop it." Very firmly she put her hands on either side of his face. "Don't say anything you might regret. Remember, I'm an officer of the court."

"I wouldn't regret it." He tugged her upward until she was sitting beside him. They were circled, he realized, by the tattered remains of her clothes. "And I don't regret this—except for the unrefined style."

She let out an impatient breath. "Look, if you can't take a joke, learn to."

"Wait until I'm finished before you swipe at me, okay? I swear, you come on faster than a typhoon." He tucked her hair back and kissed her once, hard. "I wasn't going to stay. Not today. I figured a bout of hot sex wasn't the best encore after you'd been stran-gled."

"I wasn't—"

He interrupted her. "Close enough. You know that I wanted you however I could get you, Rachel. I sure as hell didn't make a secret of it. But it occurs to me that you were upset and vulnerable and I took advan-tage of that."

She had to wait nearly a full minute before she could speak. "Don't make me mad at you, Muldoon. And don't insult me."

"All I'm trying to say is . . . I don't know what the hell I'm trying to say," he muttered, and tried again. "Except—well, maybe I could have pulled that stu-pid couch out instead of using the floor."

Eyes narrowed, she leaned her face close to his. Her eyes were the color of gold doubloons, and just as ex-otic. "I like the floor. Get it?"

He was starting to feel better. Zack knew that tend-ing to fragility was out of his league. But this tough, hardheaded woman was just his style. Watching her, he picked up her ruined blouse. "I ripped your clothes off."

"Proud of yourself?"

He tossed it aside. "Yeah. I can wait, if you want to put some more on. Then I can rip them off you again."

She bit the inside of her lip, but didn't quite defeat the smile. "Those were ruined anyway. Next time I'll have to bill you for damages. I'm on a budget."

Chuckling, he flicked her earring with his finger. "I'm crazy about you."

Her heart did a fast skip and shudder. The statement was as romantic as a whispered endearment to her. "Hey, don't get sloppy on me."

"Crazy," he said again, amazed and delighted at the faint blush that stole into her cheeks. "And did I mention that your body makes me wild?"

She was a great deal more comfortable with that. "No." She tilted her head. "Why don't you?"

"From stem to stern," he said, letting his hand speak more eloquently. "Forward and aft. Port and starboard."

"Oh, God." She gave an exaggerated sigh and shiver. "Salty talk. I just love a man out of uniform." More than willing to be aroused, she nuzzled her lips against his. "Tell me something, sailor."

"You bet."

"Which part is the stern?"

"I'll show you." Very gently, he touched his lips to her bruised throat. "Honey, we better pull that couch out before this gets out of hand again."

"Okay." There was something unspeakably erotic about a callused finger stroking the underside of her breast. "If you want."

Though the idea had merit, the couch seemed entirely too far away. "Or we could do it later. Tell you what, if you'd say something in Ukrainian, I'd forget we were on the floor. And I promise to make you forget it, too."

"Why should I say something in Ukrainian?"

"Because it drives me insane."

She tilted her head back. "Are you putting me on?"

"Uh-uh." His tongue traced a slow, teasing circle on her lips. "Go ahead. Say anything."

After a little sigh, she twined her arms around his neck. Against his ear, she murmured the words, then chuckled when he groaned.

"What did it mean?" he demanded, busying himself by nibbling his way along her shoulder.

"Loosely translated? I said you were a big, pigheaded fool."

"Mmm...are you sure you didn't say how much you wanted my body?"

"No. This is how you say that."

She told him, but by the time she was finished, he was already obliging her.

In the dark, he drew her close. They had managed, finally, to pull out the bed. Now they were tangled in her sheets. The afternoon had become evening, and evening night.

"I'd like to stay," he said quietly.

"I know." It was silly, she thought, to be unhappy that he would go. She'd always jealously prized her nights alone. "But you can't. It's too soon to trust Nick overnight."

"If things were different..." Damn, he hadn't expected it to be so frustrating. "I'd like to take you back home with me. I'd like to have you in my bed tonight, wake up with you tomorrow."

"He's not ready for that, either." She wasn't sure she was ready herself. "Until I have a chance to smooth things out with him, and make him understand, it's probably best if he doesn't know we're..."

What were they? The question ran through both their heads. Neither of them voiced it.

"You're right." The mattress creaked as he shifted. "Rachel, I want to be with you again. It doesn't just have to be in bed." He traced the curve of her cheek. "Or on the floor."

"I want to be with you." She touched her fingers to the back of his hand. "It's good. And that's enough."

"Yeah." He was nearly sure it was. "I can take some time Wednesday. How about an early dinner?"

"I'd like that." They fell into silence again, until she sighed. "You'd better go."

"I know."

"Maybe Sunday you and Nick could come to dinner at my parents'. We talked about it before, remember?"

"That would be good." He kissed her again, and the kiss went on and on. "Just once more."

"Yes." She enfolded him. "Just once more."

Rachel shifted the phone to her other ear, scribbled on a legal pad and stared dubiously at the stack of files on her desk.

"Yes, Mrs. Macetti, I understand. What we need are a couple of good character witnesses for your son. Your priest, perhaps, or a teacher." As she listened to the rapid-fire broken English, she wondered if she could catch the attention of any of her harried co-workers and hope that they'd feel sorry enough for her to bring her a cup of coffee. "I can't tell you that, Mrs. Macetti. Our chances are very good for a suspended sentence and probation, since Carlo wasn't driving. But the fact is, he was riding in a stolen car, and..."

She trailed off, carefully folding the page she'd written on. "Uh-huh. Well, as I explained before, it would be rather difficult to convince anyone he didn't know the car was stolen, since the locks had been sprung and the engine hot-wired." Satisfied with the shape of her paper airplane, she shot it out her door. It was as good as a note in a bottle.

"I'm sure he's a good boy, Mrs. Macetti." Rachel rolled her eyes. "Bad companions, yes. Let's hope that this experience will have him keeping his distance from the Hombres. Mrs. Macetti. Mrs. Macetti," Rachel said, trying to be firm, "I'm doing everything I can. Try to be optimistic, and I'll see you in court next week. No—no, really. I'll call you. Yes, I promise. Goodbye. Yes, absolutely. Goodbye."

Rachel hung up the phone, then dropped her head on her desk. Ten minutes of trying to deal with the frantic mother of six was as exhausting as a full day in court.

"Tough day?"

Lifting her head, Rachel spotted Nick in her doorway. He had her paper airplane in one hand, and a large paper cup in the other.

"Tough month." Her gaze locked on the steaming cup. "Tell me that's coffee."

"Light, no sugar." He stepped in and offered it. "Your note sounded desperate." As she took the first sip, he grinned. "I was coming down the hall, and it hit me in the chest. Nice form."

"I find they make excellent interoffice memos." Another sip and she felt the caffeine begin to pump through her system. "Since you saved my life, what can I do for you?"

"I was just kicking around. Thought maybe we could grab some lunch."

"I'm sorry, Nick." She gestured to the clutter on her desk. "I'm swamped."

"They don't let you eat?" Because he found he enjoyed seeing her here, entrenched in the business of justice, he eased a hip down on the corner of the desk.

"Oh, they throw us some raw meat now and again." Lord, he was flirting with her, she realized. Rachel gauged the files piled in front of her, calculated how much time she had before her meeting with the DA to bargain on a half a dozen cases. It was going to be close. "Actually, I would like to talk to you, if you have a few minutes."

"I'm on six to two tonight, so I've got plenty of minutes."

"Good." She stood, easing by him to close the door. The moment she turned back, she realized he'd taken that gesture the wrong way. His hands went to her waist. She had a moment to think that in a few years that combination of smooth moves and rough manners would devastate hordes of women. Then she managed to slip aside.

"Nick," she began, then hesitated. "Sit down." When he settled in her battered office chair, she sat behind the desk. "We're going on three weeks. I'd like to know how you're feeling."

"I'm cool."

"What I mean is, when we go back in front of Judge Beckett, it's very likely she'll give you probation—unless you make a big mistake in the meantime."

"I don't plan on mistakes." The chair creaked rustily as he leaned back. "Going to jail isn't high on my list these days."

"Glad to hear it. But she may also ask about your plans. This might be the time to start thinking about that, whether you'd like to make the situation with Zack more permanent."

"Permanent?" He gave a quick laugh. "Hey, I don't know about that. I'll probably want my own place, you know. Zack and me... well, maybe we're getting on a little better, but he cramps my style. Kind of hard to have a lady over when big brother can walk in any time." He flicked his green eyes over her face. "Know what I mean?"

An opening, she thought, and dived in. "Do you have a girl?"

His smile was very male and very attractive. "I'm more interested in women. Women with big brown eyes."

"Nick—"

"You know, when I was walking over here, I started to think how getting busted turned out to be a pretty lucky break." He lifted her hand, brushing his thumb over her knuckles before toying with her fingers. His eyes never left hers. "Otherwise, I wouldn't have needed such a great-looking lawyer."

"Nick, I'm twenty-six." It wasn't what she'd meant to say, or how she'd meant to say it, but he only tilted his head.

"Yeah? So?"

"And I'm your court-appointed guardian."

"Kind of an interesting situation." His smile spread. "It'll be over in about five weeks."

"I'll still be seven years older than you."

"More like six," he said easily. "But who's counting?"

"I am." Frustrated, she started to rise, then realized it would be best if she stayed in the position of authority behind the desk. "Nick, I like you, very much. And I meant what I said when I told you I wanted to be your friend."

"You can't let the age thing bother you, babe." When he rose, she realized she'd miscalculated by staying behind the desk. When he came around to sit on the edge of it, she was trapped between him and the wall.

"Of course I can. I was in college when you were starting puberty."

"Well, I've finished now." He grinned and traced his finger down her cheek. And his eyes narrowed. "Is that a bruise?"

"I ran into something," she said, and tried again. "The bottom line is, I'm too old for you."

He frowned at the bruise another minute, then lifted his eyes to hers. "I don't think so. Let me put it this way. Do you figure a woman shouldn't get tangled up with a guy six years older than she is?"

"That's entirely different."

"Sexist," he said clucking his tongue. "Here I figured you'd be all for equal rights."

"Of course I am, but—" She broke off with a hiss of breath.

"Gotcha."

"Regardless of age—" since that wasn't working, she thought "—I'm your guardian, and it would be wrong, certainly unethical, for me to encourage or agree to anything beyond that. I care about what happens to you, and if I've given you the impression that I'm interested in anything more than friendship, I'm sorry."

He considered. "I guess you take your work pretty seriously."

"Yes, I do."

"I can dig it. No pressure, right?"

Relief made her sigh. "Right." She rose, giving his hand a quick squeeze. "You're all right, Nick."

"You too." They both looked around when her phone began to shrill. "I'll let you get back to serving justice," he told her, then had her mouth dropping open as he brought her hand to his lips. "Five weeks isn't so long to wait."

"But—"

"Catch you later." He strolled out, leaving Rachel wondering if it would help to beat her head against the wall.

Nick was feeling great. He had the whole day ahead of him, money in his pocket, and a gorgeous woman planted in his heart. He had to grin when he thought about the way he'd flustered her. He hadn't realized it could be so satisfying to make a woman nervous.

And imagine a knockout like Rachel worrying about her age. Shaking his head, he jogged down to the subway. Maybe he'd thought she was a couple of years younger, but it didn't matter one way or the other. Everything about her was dead-on perfect.

He wondered how Zack would react when he saw Nick LeBeck strut into the bar one night with Rachel on his arm. He didn't imagine Zack would think of him as a kid when everybody saw he'd bagged a babe like Rachel Stanislaski.

Wrong, he told himself as he hopped on a car that would take him to Times Square. That was no way to talk about a classy lady. What they'd have was a relationship. As the subway car rattled and squeaked, he occupied himself by daydreaming about what they'd do together.

There would be dinners and long walks, quiet talks. They'd go listen to music, and dance. Now and again they'd have a lazy evening snuggled up in front of the television.

Nick considered it a sign of his commitment that he hadn't put sex at the top of the list.

On top of the world, he came out into the bustle and blare of Times Square and decided to use some of his loose change for a little pinball.

The arcade was noisy, and there was a loud rock backbeat blasting over the metallic sounds of beeps and buzzes. Though he'd missed the freedom of being able to breeze into an arcade any time he chose, he had to admit it felt good to be able to spend money he'd earned.

No sneaking around, no vague sense of guilt. Maybe he didn't have the gang to hang around with, but he didn't feel nearly as lonely as he'd thought he would.

It wasn't something he'd admit out loud, but he was getting a kick out of working in the kitchen with Rio. The big cook had plenty of stories, many of them about Zack. When he listened to them, Nick almost felt as though he'd been part of it.

Of course, he hadn't, Nick reminded himself, using expert body English to play out the ball. There was no possible way he could explain how miserable he'd been when Zack shipped out. Then he'd had no one again. His mother had tried, he supposed, but she'd always been more shadow than substance in his life.

It had taken all her energy to put food on the table and clothes on his back. She'd had little of herself left over once that was done.

Then there had been Zack.

Nick could still remember the first time he'd seen his stepbrother. In the kitchen of the bar. Zack had been sitting at the counter, gobbling potato chips. He'd been tall and dark, with an easy grin and a casually generous manner. Once Nick had gotten up the courage to follow him around, Zack hadn't tried to shake him off.

It was Zack who'd brought him into an arcade the first time, propped him up and shown him how to make the silver balls dance.

It was Zack who'd taken him to the Macy's parade. Zack who had patiently taught him to tie his shoes. Zack who'd clobbered him when he chased a ball into traffic.

And it was Zack who, barely a year later, had left him with a sick mother and an overbearing stepfather. Postcards and souvenirs hadn't filled the hole.

Maybe Zack wanted to make up for it, Nick thought with a shrug, then swore when the ball slipped by the flipper. And maybe, deep down, Nick wanted to let him.

"Hey, LeBeck." The slap on his shoulder nearly made Nick lose the next ball. "Where you been hiding?"

"I've been around." Nick sliced a quick glance at Cash before concentrating on his game. He wondered if Cash would make any comment about him not wearing his Cobra jacket.

"Yeah? Thought you'd dropped down the sewer." Cash leaned against the machine, as always, appreciating Nick's skill. "Haven't lost your touch."

"I've got great hands. Ask the babes."

Cash snorted and lighted a crushed cigarette. His last. Since Reece had copped less than ten cents on the dollar for the stolen merchandise, Cash's share was long gone. "Man, the chicks see that ugly face and you never get a chance to use your hands."

"You've got your butt mixed up with my face." Nick eased back on his heels, satisfied with his score and the free game he'd finessed. "Want to take this one?"

"Sure." After stepping behind the machine, Cash began to bull his way through the game. "You still hanging with your stepbrother?"

"Yeah, got a few more weeks before we go back to court."

Cash lost the first ball and pumped up another. "You got a tough break, Nick. I mean that, man. I feel real bad about the way it went down."

"Right."

"No, man. Really." In his sincerity, Cash lost track of the ball and let it slip away. "We screwed up, and you took the heat."

Slightly mollified, Nick shrugged. "I can handle it."

"Still sucks. But hey, it can't be so bad working a bar. Plenty of juice, right?"

Nick smiled. He wasn't about to admit he'd downed no more than two beers in the past three weeks. And if Zack got wind of that much, there'd be hell to pay. "You got it, bro."

"I guess the place does okay, right? I mean, it's popular and all."

"Does okay."

"Must be plenty of sexy ladies dropping in, looking for action."

The neighborhood bar ran more to blue-collar workers and families, but Nick played along. "The place is lousy with them. It's pick and choose."

Cash laughed appreciatively even as he blew his last ball. "Want to go doubles?"

"Why not?" Nick dug in his pocket for more tokens. "So what's going on with the gang?"

"The usual. T.J.'s old man kicked him out, so he's bunking with me. Jerk snores like a jackhammer."

"Man, don't I know it. I put up with him a couple of nights last summer."

"Couple of the Hombres crossed over to our turf. We handled them."

Nick knew that meant fists, maybe chains and bottles. Occasionally blades. It was odd, he thought, but all that seemed so distant to him, distant and useless. "Yeah, well..." was all he could think of to say.

"Some people never learn, you know. Got a cigarette? I'm tapped."

"Yeah, top pocket." Nick racked up another ten thousand points while Cash lit up.

"Hey, I got a connection at this strip joint downtown. Could get you in."

"Yeah?" Nick answered absently as he sent the ball bouncing.

"Sure. I'd like to make that other business up to you. Maybe I'll drop by one night and we'll hang out."

"Forget it."

"No, man, really. I'll spring for the brew, too. Don't tell me slippery LeBeck can't slip out."

"I can get out when I want. Just walk out the kitchen."

"Around the back?"

"Yeah. Zack's usually tied up at the bar until three. Two on Sundays. I can get around Rio when I want to, or take the fire escape."

"You got a place upstairs?"

"Mmm . . . Your ball."

When they switched positions, Cash continued to question him, making it casual. The cash went in a safe in the office. Business usually peaked by one on Wednesdays. There were three ways in. The front door, the back, and through the upstairs apartment.

By the time Nick had trounced him three games in a row, Cash had all he needed. He made his excuses and wandered out to meet with Reece.

He didn't feel good about conning Nick. But he *was* a Cobra.

Chapter Eight

Zack stepped out of the shower, grateful the endless afternoon was over. He didn't mind paperwork. Or at least he didn't hate it. Well, the truth was, he hated it, but accepted that it was a necessary evil.

He'd made his orders, paid his invoices and tallied his end-of-the-month figures. Well, maybe he was a week or so behind the end of the month, but still, he figured he was doing pretty well.

And so was the business.

It looked as though he'd finally pulled it out of the hole his father's illness and the resulting expenses had dug. Paying off the loan he'd taken to square things for Nick would pinch a little, but in another year he'd be able to do more than look at boats in catalogs.

He wondered how Rachel would feel about taking a month off and sailing down to the Caribbean. He liked to imagine her lying out on the polished deck, wearing some excuse for a bikini. He liked the idea of watching her hair blow around her face when it caught the wind.

Of course, he'd have to take some time to check the boat out, test the rigging. He thought he'd be able to talk Nick into a day sail, or maybe a weekend. He wanted the two of them to be able to get away—away from the bar, the city, and the memories that tied them to both.

With a towel slung around his hips, he walked to the bedroom to dress. He hoped, sincerely, that the Sunday dinner at the Stanislaskis' would crack the kid's defenses a little more. Whenever Rachel spoke about her family, it made him think of what they—of what Nick—had missed.

All the kid needed was a little time to see how things could be. They were nearly halfway through the trial run, and apart from a few skirmishes, it had gone smoothly enough.

He had Rachel to thank for that, Zack thought as he tugged on a pair of jeans. He had Rachel to thank for a lot of things. Not only had she given him a second chance with Nick, but she'd added something incredible to his life. Something he'd never expected to have. Something he'd—

On a long breath, he stared hard into the mirror. When a man was going down for the third time, he recognized the signs.

Don't be an idiot, Muldoon, he told his reflection. Keep it steady as she goes. The lady wants to keep it simple, and so do you.

It wouldn't do to forget it.

"Hot date?" Feigning disinterest, Nick slouched against the doorjamb. He'd been passing and had caught the way Zack was staring blindly into the mirror.

"Huh? Yeah, I guess you could say that." Nick dragged a hand through his wet hair and scattered drops of water. "I didn't know you were back."

"I'm on at six." For reasons Nick couldn't understand, he was swamped by the memory of the times he'd stood in the bathroom watching Zack shave. How it had made him feel when Zack slapped shaving cream on his face. "Rio's got beef stew on special tonight. Too bad you'll miss it."

Zack grabbed a shirt. "You take my share or Rio'll make me eat it for breakfast."

Nick grinned, then remembered himself and smirked. "You take a lot of crap from him."

"He's bigger than I am."

"Yeah, right."

Watching Nick in the mirror, Zack buttoned his shirt. "He likes to think he's looking out for me. It doesn't cost me anything to let him. He ever tell you about how he got that scar down the side of his face?"

"He said something about a broken bottle and a drunk marine."

"The drunk marine was going for my throat with that broken bottle. Rio got in his way. The way I see it, I owe Rio a lot more than putting up with his nagging." Tucking in his shirt, Zack turned, grinned. "And you're getting paid to put up with it."

"He's okay." Nick would have liked to ask more, like why a drunk marine had wanted to slice Zack's throat, but he was afraid Zack would just shrug it off.

"Listen, if you get lucky tonight, don't worry about coming back."

Zack's fingers paused on the snap of his jeans. Tucking his tongue in his cheek, he wondered how Rachel would take his brother's turn of phrase. "Thanks for the thought, but I'll be home."

"For bed check," Nick muttered.

"Call it what you want," Zack shot back, then bit off an oath. Come hell or high water, they were going to get through one conversation without raised voices. "Listen, I don't figure you're going to climb out the window. Hell, you could do that while I'm here. It could be the lady won't want company overnight."

Mollified, Nick hooked his thumbs in his pockets. "They didn't teach you a hell of a lot in the navy, did they, bro?"

In an old gesture they'd both nearly forgotten, Zack rubbed his knuckles over Nick's head. "Kiss my butt." With his jacket slung over his shoulder, he headed out. "And don't wait up. I'm feeling lucky."

Long after the door shut behind Zack, Nick was still grinning.

Rachel was just unlocking the outside door when Zack strode up behind her. "Good timing," he said, and pressed a kiss to the back of her neck.

"For you, maybe. Everything ran over today. I was hoping to get back and soak in the tub before you got here."

"You want to soak?" The minute they were in the elevator, he had her against the wall. "Go ahead. I'll scrub your back."

"What a guy." When his mouth closed over hers, it hurt, somewhere deep, reminding her just how much she'd wanted to be with him again. "You smell good."

"Must be these." He pulled a paper cone filled with roses from behind his back.

Her heart wanted to sigh, but she resisted. "Another bribe?" She couldn't resist the urge to bury her face in the blooms.

"There was a guy selling them a couple of blocks down. He looked like he could use a couple bucks."

"Softy." She handed him her keys so that he could unlock her door and she could continue to sniff the roses.

"Keep it to yourself."

"It'll cost you." After kicking the door closed with her foot, she dumped her briefcase and laid the spray of roses on a table. "Pay up, Muldoon," she demanded, tossing her arms around him.

There was such joy in it. Heat, yes. And the sweet, sharp ache of need. But the joy was so unexpected, so fast and full, that she laughed against his mouth as he twirled her around.

"I missed you." He continued to hold her, inches off the floor.

"Oh, yeah?" With her hands linked comfortably around his neck, she smiled. "Maybe I missed you, too. Some. How long are you going to hold me up here?"

"This way I can look right at you. You're beautiful, Rachel."

It wasn't the words so much as the way he said them that brought a lump to her throat. "You don't have to soften me up."

"I don't know how to tell you how beautiful—except that sometimes when I look at you, I remember how the sea looks, right at sunrise, when all that color spills out of the sky, kind of seeps over the horizon and falls into the water. Just for a few minutes, everything's so vivid, so... I don't know, special. When I look at you, it's like that."

Her eyes had darkened with an emotion she couldn't begin to analyze. All she could do was rest her cheek against his. "Zack." His name was a sigh, and she knew she would cry any minute if she didn't lighten the mood. "Roses and poetry, all in one day. I don't know what to say to you."

Enchanted, he buried his face in her hair. "That's a first."

"We're not going to get—"

"Sloppy," he finished for her, laughing. "Us? Are you kidding?" But when he sat on the couch, he kept her cuddled in his lap. "Let me see that bruise."

"It's nothing," she said, even as he tilted her head for a closer inspection. "The worst of it was that the word got out and I had to deal with all this sympathy and advice. If those cops had kept their mouths shut, I could have said I'd walked into a door."

"Take off the jacket and sweater."

She arched a brow. "You're such a romantic, Muldoon."

"Can it. I want to see your neck."

"It's fine."

"Which is why you're wearing a sweater that comes up to your chin."

"It's very fashionable."

"Peel it off, babe, or I'll have to do it for you."

Her eyes lit. "Ah, threatening a public official."
After kicking off her shoes, she tossed up her chin.
"Try it, Buster. Let's see how tough you are."

She didn't put up much of a fight, but the initial
wrestling was enough to arouse them both. By the time
he had her pinned to the couch, her arms over her
head and her wrists cuffed in his hand, they were both
breathing hard.

"I took it easy on you," she told him.

"I could see that." Her jacket was crumpled on the
floor beside them. Smiling, Zack began to inch her
sweater upward, letting his fingers skim over the silky
material beneath.

Her breath caught, and released unsteadily. "That's
not my neck," she managed as his hand cupped and
molded her breast.

"Just checking." Watching her, always watching
her, he teased the nipple until it was hot and hard.
"You're quick to the touch, Rachel."

His touch, she thought, trembling. Only his.

Slowly, determined to savor every moment, he
slipped the sweater up. He released her wrists to tug it
off, then clasped them again.

"Zack."

He ignored her flexing hands. "My turn at the
helm," he said quietly. "I told you once I wanted to
drive you crazy. Do you remember?"

He was. He already was. "I want to touch you."

"You will." He skimmed a fingertip over her neck
first, carefully studying the bruises. They were fading
to yellow. "I don't want to see you hurt again." Gently
he lowered his head to trail a necklace of kisses over
the marks. "Not ever again."

"It doesn't hurt." Her pulse jackhammered under his nuzzling lips. "I don't need to be seduced."

"Yes, you do. But you're afraid to be, which makes the whole idea damn near irresistible. You're just going to have to trust me." He shifted so that he could unzip her skirt and slip it off. "I have places to take you." His mouth lowered to hers, rubbing, then nibbling. "Strange, wonderful places." Then diving deep.

The journey wasn't calm, but she had no choice but to go where he took her. This eagerness for pleasure, this immediacy of need, was still so new that she had no defense against it. His hand slid over her, lingering here, exploiting there, while his mouth devoured hers with a relentless hunger.

No escape, she thought desperately as he brought her close, painfully close, to that first tumultuous release. She was trapped in him, utterly lost in a tangled maze of sensations. She writhed beneath his hand, too steeped in her own needs to know how deliciously wanton her movements were.

"I didn't have time to appreciate these last time." Zack trailed his fingers up the sheer stocking to the pristine white garter. She would think them practical, he knew. He thought them erotic.

With an expert flick of his fingers that had her moaning, he released one stocking, then the other, before tormenting them both by peeling them, inch by lazy inch, down her legs.

He had to kneel on the floor to taste her calves, the backs of her knees, the glorious satin skin of her thighs. She cried out when he slid his tongue beneath her panties to sample the hot, sensitive flesh underneath. Fighting impatience, he tugged them off to give himself the freedom to taste more of her.

As the first wave swamped her, she arched like a bow, leaping into Ukrainian when the aftershocks shuddered through her. Freed, her hands groped for him until they were struggling together to strip off his clothes. Heat to heat, she pressed against him, over-balancing him, until she straddled him and her mouth could merge hotly with his.

"Now." was all he said, all he *could* say, as he gripped her hips.

"I really did mean to take you out," Zack said when they lay on the couch in a tangle of limbs.

"I bet."

He smiled, recognized the sleepy satisfaction in her voice. "Really. We can get dressed and try again."

With a half laugh, she pressed her lips to his chest. His heart was still thundering. "You're not going anywhere, Muldoon. Not till I'm finished with you."

"If you insist."

"That's what free delivery's for. How about Chinese?"

"You're on. Who's going to get up and call?"

She shifted for the pleasure of rubbing her cheek against his skin. "We'll flip for it."

He lost, and Rachel took advantage of the moment to grab a quick, bracing shower. When she came back, her hair damp and curly, a plain white terry-cloth robe skimming her knees, he was pouring them both a glass of wine.

"I think I'm repeating myself," he said, offering her a glass. "But you sure look good wet."

He'd tugged on his jeans, but hadn't bothered with his shirt. Rachel trailed a finger down his chest. "You could have joined me."

"We'd have missed the delivery boy."

"Since he's bringing egg rolls, you have a point." She moved to the kitchen to get some plates, then set them on the table by the window. "And I do have to refuel. I only had time for a candy bar at lunch." Because the mood seemed right, she lit candles. "Nick dropped by the office."

"Oh."

"I wish I had had more time...." She touched match to wick and watched the candle flare. "He caught me between phone calls and before a plea-bargaining meeting."

He watched her move around the room in her practical terry-cloth robe, turning the light into romance with her candles. He wondered if she realized how compelling that contrast was. "You don't have to explain to me, Rachel."

She shook out a match, struck another. It wasn't that she was superstitious, but there was no use taking chances with three on a match. "I have to explain to myself. He wanted to go to lunch, and I just couldn't swing it. I did talk to him about ... the situation."

"About the fact that he's fallen in lust with you."

"I wouldn't put it like that." She sighed heavily when the intercom buzzed. After flipping it on, she released the security lock for the delivery boy. "He's simply misinterpreted gratitude and friendship."

Zack took one long look at her in the candleglow. "Whatever you say."

Disgusted, she went back to the table and sat. "You're buying, Muldoon."

He took out his wallet agreeably. He had the tab and the tip ready when the delivery arrived. After carrying three bulging bags to the table, he unpacked the little white cartons. In moments the air was filled with exotic aromas.

"Do you want to tell me the rest?"

"Well..." Rachel wound some noodles around her chopsticks. "I started off explaining the difference in our ages. Umm..." She chewed appreciatively. "He didn't buy it," she said over a mouthful. "He had a very convincing argument, and since I couldn't override it, I changed tactics."

"I've seen you in court," he reminded her.

"I explained the ethics of my being his guardian, and how it wasn't possible for us to go beyond those terms." Thoughtful, she scooped up some sweet and sour pork. "He seemed to understand that."

"Good."

"I thought it was. I mean, he agreed with me. He was very mature about it. Then, when he was leaving, he said how it wasn't so hard to wait five more weeks."

Zack said nothing for a moment. Then, with a half laugh, he picked up his wine. "You've got to give the kid credit."

"Zack, this is serious."

"I know. I know. It's sticky for both of us, but you have to admire the way he turned it around on you."

"I told you he was smooth." After peeking in another carton, she nibbled on some chilled chicken and bean sprouts. "Don't you know any nice teenage girls you could nudge in his direction?"

"Lola's got one," Zack said, considering. "I think she's sixteen."

"Lola has a teenager?"

"Three of them. She likes to say she started young so that she could lose her mind before she turned forty. I can feel her out about it."

"It couldn't hurt. I'm going to try again, though I'm hoping the feeling will pass in another week or two."

"I wouldn't count on it." Reaching across the table, he linked his fingers with hers. "You stick in a man's mind."

"Does that mean you're thinking of me when you're mixing drinks and flirting with the customers?"

"I never flirt with Pete."

She laughed. "I was thinking more of those two 'babes' who drop in. The blonde and the redhead. They always order stingers."

"You are observant, Counselor."

"The redhead's got her big green eyes on you."

"They're blue."

"A-ha!"

He shook his head, amazed he'd fallen so snugly into the trap. "It pays to know your regulars. Besides, I like brown eyes—especially when they lean toward gold."

She let his lips brush hers. "Too late." With her head close to his, she laughed again. "It's all right, Muldoon. I can always borrow Rio's meat cleaver if you notice more than her eyes."

"Then I'm safe. I've never paid any attention to those cute little freckles over her nose. Or that sexy dimple in her chin."

Eyes narrowed, Rachel bit his lip. "Get any lower, and you'll be in deep water."

"That's okay. I'm a strong swimmer."

Hours later, when Zack crawled into a cold, empty bed, he warmed himself by thinking of it. It had been nice, just nice, to laugh together over the cardboard boxes and chopsticks. They'd sampled each other's choices, talking while the candles had burned low. Not about Nick, not about work, but about dozens of other things.

Then they'd made love again, slowly, sweetly, while the night grew late around them.

He'd had to leave her. He had responsibilities. But as he settled his body toward sleep, he let his mind wander, imagining what it could be like.

Waking up with her. Feeling her stretch against him as the alarm rang. Watching her. Smiling to himself as she hurried around the apartment, getting dressed for work.

She'd be wearing one of those trim suits while they stood in the kitchen sharing coffee, talking over their plans for the day.

Sometimes they'd steal a quick lunch together, because they both hated to have a whole day pass without touching. When he could, he'd slip away from work so that he could walk home with her in the evening. When he couldn't, he'd look forward to seeing her come through the door, slide onto a stool at the bar, where she'd eat Rio's chili and flirt with him.

Then they would go home together.

One balmy weekend they would set sail together. He'd teach her how to man the tiller. They'd glide out over blue water, with the sails billowing....

The waves were high as mountains, rearing up to slap viciously at the ship. The bellow of the wind was like a thousand women screaming. Burying a fear that he knew could be as destructive as the gale, he scrambled over the pitching deck, clinging to the slippery rail as he shouted orders.

The rain was lashing his face like a whip, blinding him. His red-rimmed eyes stung from the salt water. He knew the boat was out there—radar had it—but all he could see was wall after wall of deadly water.

The next wave swamped the deck, sucking at him. Lightning cracked the sky like a bullet through glass. The ship heeled. He saw the seaman tumble, heard the shout as his hands scrambled on the deck for purchase. Zack leaped, snagging a sleeve, then a wrist.

A line. For God's sake, get me a line.

And he was dragging the dead weight back from the rail.

Wind and water. Wind and water.

There, in a flash of lightning, was the disabled boat. Lower the tow line. Make it fast. As the lightning stuttered against the dark, he could see three figures. They'd lashed themselves on—a man to the wheel, a woman behind him, a young girl to the mast.

They were fighting, valiantly, but a forty-foot boat was no match for the fury of a hurricane at sea. It was impossible to send out a launch. He had to hope one of them could hold the boat steady while another secured the tow.

Signal lights flashed instructions through the storm.

It happened fast. Another spear of lightning, and the mast cracked, falling like a tree under an ax. Horrified, he watched the young girl being dragged with it into the swirling water.

No time to think. Pure instinct had Zack grabbing a flotation device and diving into the face of the storm.

Falling, falling, endlessly, while the gale tumbled his body like dice in a gambler's hand. Black, pitch-black, then the white flare of lightning. Hitting a wall of water that felt like stone. Having it close relentlessly over your head. Like death.

Zack awoke gasping for air and choking against the nightmare water. Sweat had soaked through to the sheets, making him shiver in the chill. With a groan, he let his head fall back and waited for the first grinding ache of nausea to pass.

The room tilted once as he staggered to his feet. From past experience, Zack knew to close his eyes until it righted again. Moving through the dark, he went into the bathroom to splash the cold sweat from his face.

"Hey, you okay?" Nick was hovering in the doorway. "You sick or something?"

"No." Zack cupped a hand near the faucet, catching enough water to ease his dry throat. "Go back to bed."

Nick hesitated, studying Zack's pale face. "You look sick."

"Damn it, I said I'm fine. Beat it."

Nick's eyes darkened with angry hurt before he swung away.

"Hey, wait. Sorry." Zack let out a long breath. "Nightmare. Puts me in a lousy mood."

"You had a nightmare?"

"That's what I said." Embarrassed, Zack snatched up a towel to dry off.

It was hard for Nick to imagine big, bad Zack having a nightmare, or anything else that would make him sweat and go pale. "Uh, you want a drink?"

"Yeah." Steadier now, Zack lowered the towel. "There's some of the old man's whiskey in the kitchen."

After a moment, Zack followed Nick out. He sat on the arm of a chair while Nick splashed three fingers of whiskey into a tumbler. He took it, swallowed, then hissed. "I can't figure out how he had a liver left at the end."

Nick wished he'd pulled pants over his briefs. At least he'd have had pockets to dip his hands into. "I think when he started to forget stuff, it helped him to blame it on the whiskey instead of—you know."

"Alzheimer's. Yeah." Zack took another swallow, let it lie on his tongue a moment so that his throat could get used to the idea.

"I heard you thrashing around in there. Sounded pretty bad."

"It was pretty bad." Zack tilted the glass, watched the whiskey lap this way and that. "Hurricane. One mean bitch. I never understood why they started naming them after guys, too. Take it from me, a hurricane's all woman." He let his head fall back again, let his eyes close. "It's been nearly three years, and I haven't been able to shake this lady."

"You want to—" Nick cut himself off. "That should help you sleep."

Zack knew what Nick had wanted to ask. And he did want to. It might be best for both of them if they talked it through. "We were off of Bermuda when we got the distress call. We were the closest ship, and the captain had to make a choice. We turned back into the hurricane. Three civilians in a pleasure boat. They'd been thrown off course and hadn't been able to make it to shore before the storm hit."

Saying nothing, Nick sat on the arm of the couch so that he was facing his brother.

"Seventy-five knot winds, and the seas—they must have been forty feet. I've been through a hurricane after it's made landfall. It can be bad, real bad, but it's nothing like it is when it's at sea. You don't know scared until you see something like that. Hear something like that. The lieutenant took a rap on the head, it put him out. We came close to losing some of the crew over the side. Sometimes it was black, so black you couldn't see your own hands—but you could see that water rising up. Then the lightning would hit, and blind you."

"How were you supposed to find them in all that?"

"We had them on radar. The quartermaster could've slipped that ship through the crack of dawn. He was good. We spotted them, thirty degrees off to starboard. They'd tied the kid—little girl—to the main mast. The man and woman were fighting to keep it afloat, but they were taking on water fast. We had time. I remember thinking we could pull it off. Then the mast cracked. I thought I heard the girl scream, but it was probably the wind, because she went under pretty quick. So I went in."

"You went in?" Nick repeated, wide-eyed. "You jumped in the water?"

"I was over the side before I thought about it. I wasn't being a hero, I just didn't think. Believe me, if I had..." He let the words trail off, then swallowed the rest of the whiskey. "It was like jumping off a sky-scraper. You don't think you're ever going to stop falling. It was end over end, forever, giving you plenty of time to realize you've just killed yourself. It was stupid—if the wind had been wrong it would have just smashed me against the side of the ship. But I was lucky, and it tossed me toward the boat. Then I hit. God, it was like ramming full-length into concrete."

He hadn't known until later that he'd snapped his collarbone and dislocated his left shoulder.

"I couldn't get my bearings. The water kept heaving me around, sucking me down. It was so black, the searchlight barely cut through. There I was, drown-ing, and I couldn't even remember what I was doing. It was blind luck that I found the mast. She was all tangled up in the line. I don't know how many times we went under while I was trying to get her loose. My hands were numb, and I was working blind. Then I had her, and I managed to get the flotation on her. They said I got the tow line secured, but I don't re-member. I just remember hanging on to her and wait-ing for the next wave to finish us off. Next thing, I was waking up in the infirmary. The kid was sitting there, wrapped in a blanket and holding my hand." He smiled. It helped to think about that part. Just that part. "She was one tough little monkey. A damn admiral's granddaughter."

"You saved her life."

"Maybe. For the first couple of months, I jumped off that deck every time I closed my eyes. Now it's only once or twice a year. It still scares the breath out of me."

"I didn't think you were scared of anything."

"I'm scared of plenty," Zack said quietly as he met his brother's eyes. "For a while I was scared I wouldn't be able to stand on deck and look out at the water again. I was scared to come back here, knowing that once I did, my whole life was going to change. And I'm scared of ending up like the old man, sick and feeble and used up. I guess I'm scared you're going to walk out that door in a few weeks, feeling the same about me you did when you walked in."

Nick broke the gaze first, staring over Zack's shoulder at the shadowy wall. "I don't know how I feel. You came back because you had to. I stayed because there was no place else to go."

There was no arguing with the truth. As far as Zack could see, Nick had summed it up perfectly. "We never had much of a shot before."

"You didn't hang around very long."

"I couldn't get along with the old man—"

"You were the only one he cared about," Nick blurted out. "Every day I'd have to hear about how great you were, how you were making something out of yourself. What a hero you were. And how I was nothing." He caught himself, swallowed the need. "But that's cool. You were his blood, and I was just something that got dumped on him when my mother died.''

"He didn't feel that way. He didn't," Zack insisted. "For God's sake, Nick, when I lived with him, he was never satisfied with me, either. I was here, and my mother wasn't. That was enough to make him miserable every time he looked at me. Hell, he didn't mean it." Zack closed his eyes and missed the flicker of surprise that passed over Nick's face. "It was just the way he was. It took me years to realize he was always on my back because it was the only way he knew to be a father. It was the same with you."

"He wasn't my..." But this time Nick trailed off without finishing the sentence, or the thought.

"Toward the end, he asked for you. He really wanted to see you, Nick. Most of the times he came around like that, he thought you were still a little kid. And sometimes—most times, really—he just got the two of us mixed up together. Then he'd yell at me for both of us." He said it with a smile—a smile that Nick didn't return. "I'm not blaming you for staying away, or for holding all those years of criticism and complaints against him. I understand that it was too late for him, Nick. It doesn't have to be too late for you."

"What does it matter to you?"

"You're all the family I've got." He rose and laid a hand on Nick's shoulder, relaxing when it wasn't shoved off. "Maybe, when it comes right down to the bottom line, you're all the family I've ever had. I don't want to lose that."

"I don't know how to be family," Nick murmured.

"Me either. Maybe we can figure it out together."

Nick glanced up, then away. "Maybe. We're stuck with each other a few more weeks, anyway."

It would do, Zack thought as he gave Nick's shoulder a quick squeeze. It would do for now. "Thanks for the drink, kid. Do me a favor and don't mention the nightmare business to anyone."

"I can dig it." Nick watched Zack start back toward the bedroom. "Zack?"

"Yeah."

He didn't know what he wanted to say—just that it felt good, that he felt good. "Nothing. Night."

"Good night." Zack eased back into bed with a sigh, certain he'd sleep like a baby.

Chapter Nine

Something had changed. Rachel couldn't put her finger on it, but as she sat between Zack and Nick on the subway to Brooklyn she knew there was something going on between them. Something different.

It made her nerves hum. It made her wonder if she'd made a mistake in bringing the problems of the men who flanked her into her parents' home.

And her problem, as well, she admitted. After all, she wouldn't deny she cared about both of them more than what could be considered professional. She felt a kinship with Nick—the younger-sibling syndrome, she supposed. Added to that, she'd been telling the simple truth when she confessed to Zack that she had a weakness for bad boys.

She wanted to do more for Nick LeBeck than help him stay out of jail.

As for Nick's big brother, she'd long since crossed all professional boundaries with him, into what could only be termed a full-blown affair. Even sitting beside him in the rumbling car, she thought about the last time they'd been together, alone. And it took no effort at all to imagine what it would be like the next time they could steal a few hours.

Her mother was bound to sense it, Rachel mused. Nothing got past Nadia Stanislaski when it came to her children. She wondered what her mother would think of him. What she would think of the fact that her baby girl had taken a lover.

For two people who had vowed not to complicate matters, she and Zack had done a poor job of it, Rachel decided. She'd been so certain she could keep her priorities well in line, accept the physical aspects of a relationship with a man she liked and respected without dwelling on the thorny issue of what-happens-next.

But she was thinking about Zack too much, already slotting herself as part of a couple when she'd always been perfectly content to go along single.

Now, when she imagined moving along without him, the picture turned dull and listless.

Her problem, Rachel reminded herself. After all, they had made a pact, and she never went back on her word. It was something she would have to deal with when the time came. Much more immediate was the nagging sensation that the relationship of the men beside her had taken a fast turn without her being aware of it.

To offset the feeling, she kept up a steady stream of conversation until they reached their stop.

"It's only a few blocks," Rachel said, dragging her hair back as a brisk autumn wind swirled around them. "I hope you don't mind the walk."

Zack lifted a brow. "I think we can handle it. You seem nervous, Rachel. She seem nervous to you, Nick?"

"Pretty jumpy."

"That's ridiculous." She headed into the wind, and the men fell in beside her.

"It's probably the thought of having a criminal type sit down to Sunday dinner," Zack commented. "Now she's going to have to count all the silverware."

Shocked at the statement, Rachel started to respond, but Nick merely snorted and answered for himself. "If you ask me, she's worried about inviting some Irish sailor. She has to worry if he'll drink all the booze and pick a fight."

"I can handle my liquor, pal. And I don't plan on picking a fight. Unless it's with the cop."

Nick crunched a dry leaf as it skittered across the sidewalk. "I'll take the cop."

Why, they're *joking* with each other, Rachel realized. Like brothers. Very much like brothers. Delighted, she linked arms with both of them. "If either of you takes on Alex, you'll be in for a surprise. He's meaner than he looks. And the only thing I'm nervous about is that I won't get my share of dinner. I've seen both of you eat."

"This from a woman who packs it away like a linebacker."

Rachel narrowed her eyes at Zack. "I merely have a healthy appetite."

He grinned down at her. "Me too, sugar."

She was wondering how to control the sudden leap of her heart rate when a car skidded to a halt in the street beside them. "Hey!" the driver called out.

"Hey back." Rachel broke away to walk over to greet her brother and sister-in-law. Bending into the tiny window of the MG, she kissed Mikhail and smiled at his wife. "Still keeping him in line, Sydney?"

Cool and elegant beside her untamed-looking husband, Sydney smiled. "Absolutely. Difficult jobs are my forte."

Mikhail pinched his wife's thigh and nodded toward the sidewalk. "So what's the story there?"

"They're my guests." She gave Mikhail a long, warning look that she knew was wasted on him before calling to Nick and Zack. "Come meet my brother and his long-suffering wife. Sydney, Mikhail, this is Zackary Muldoon and Nicholas LeBeck."

His eyes shielded by dark glasses, Mikhail took a careful survey. He had a brother's natural lack of faith in his sister's judgment. "Which is the client?"

"Today," Rachel said, "they're both guests."

Sydney leaned over and jammed her elbow sharply in Mikhail's ribs. "It's very nice to meet you, both of you. You're in for quite a treat with Nadia's cooking."

"So I hear." Zack kept his eyes on Mikhail as he answered, and lifted a proprietary hand to Rachel's shoulder.

Mikhail's fingers drummed on the steering wheel. "You own what? A bar?"

"No, actually, I'm into white slavery."

That got a chuckle from Nick before Rachel shook her head. "Go park your car."

As they retreated to the sidewalk, Nick smiled over at Rachel. "I see what you mean now about older brothers. Being a pain must go with the position."

"Responsibility," Zack told him. "We just pass on the benefit of our experience."

"No," Rachel said, "what you are is nosy." Amused, she gestured toward the sound of voices and laughter. Mikhail and Sydney were already at the door of the row house, hugging and being hugged. "This is it." When Rachel spotted Natasha, she gave a cry of pleasure and dashed up the steps.

Hanging back a little, Zack watched Rachel embrace her sister. Natasha was slighter, more delicately built, with rich brown eyes misted with tears, and tumbled raven curls raining down her back. Zack's first thought was that this could not be the mother of three Rachel had described to him. Then a young boy of six or seven squeezed between the women and demanded attention.

"You let in the cold!" This was bellowed from inside the house in a rumbling male voice that carried to the sidewalk and beyond. "You are not born in barn."

"Yes, Papa." Her voice sounded meek enough, but Rachel winked at her nephew as she lifted him up for a kiss. "My sister, Natasha," she continued, as they stood in the open doorway. "And my boyfriend, Brandon. And," she said when a toddler wandered up to hang on Natasha's legs, "Katie."

"You pick me up," Katie demanded, homing in on Nick. "Okay?" She was already holding up her arms, smiling flirtatiously. Nick cleared his throat and glanced at Rachel for help. When he only got a smile and a shrug, he bent down awkwardly.

"Sure. I guess."

An expert at such matters, Katie settled herself on his hip and wound an arm around his neck.

"She enjoys men," Natasha explained. When her father bellowed again, she rolled her eyes. "Come inside, please."

Zack was struck by the sounds and the scents. Home, he realized. This was a home. And stepping inside made him realize he'd never really had one himself.

The scents of ham and cloves and furniture polish, the clash of mixed voices. The carpet on the stairway leading to the second floor was worn at the edges, testimony to the dozens of feet that had climbed up or down. The furniture in the cramped living room was faded with sun and time, crowded now with people. A gleaming piano stood against one wall. Atop it was a bronze sculpture. He recognized the faces of Rachel's family, melded together, cheek to cheek, flanked by two older, proud faces that could only be her parents'.

He didn't know much about art, but he understood that this represented a unity that could not be broken.

"So you bring your friends, then leave them in the cold." Yuri sat in an armchair, cuddling a sprite of a girl. His big workingman's arms nearly enveloped the pretty child, who had a fairy's blond hair and curious eyes.

"It's only a little cold." Rachel bent to kiss her father, then the girl. "Freddie, you get prettier every time I see you."

Freddie smiled and tried to pretend she wasn't staring at the young blond man who was holding her little sister. But she had just turned thirteen, and whole worlds were opening up to her.

Rachel went through another round of introductions. Freddie turned the name Nick LeBeck over in her head while Yuri shouted out orders.

"Alexi, bring hot cider. Rachel, take coats upstairs. Mikhail, kiss your wife later. Go tell Mama we have company."

Within moments, Zack found himself seated on the couch, scratching the ears of a big, floppy dog named Ivan and discussing the pros and cons of running a business with Yuri.

Nick felt desperately self-conscious with a baby on his knee. She didn't seem to be in any hurry to get down. And the little blond girl named Freddie kept studying him with solemn gray eyes. He glanced away, wishing their mother would come along and do something. Anything. Katie snuggled up and began to toy with his earring.

"Pretty," she said, with a smile so sweet he couldn't help but respond. "I have earrings, too. See?" To show off her tiny gold hoops, she turned her head this way and that. "'Cause I'm Daddy's little gypsy."

"I bet." Unconsciously he lifted a hand to stroke her hair. "You kind of look like your Aunt Rachel."

"I can take her." Freddie had worked up her courage and now she stood beside the couch smiling down at Nick. "If she's bothering you."

Nick merely moved his shoulders. "She's cool." He struggled to find something to say. The girl was china-doll pretty, he thought, and as foreign to him as

Rachel's Ukraine. "Uh . . . you don't look a whole lot like sisters."

Freddie's smile bloomed warm and her fledgling woman's heart tapped a little faster. *He'd noticed her.* "Mama's my stepmother, technically. I was about six when she and my father got married."

"Oh." A *step,* he thought. That was something he knew about, and sympathized with. "I guess it was a little rough on you."

Though she was baffled, Freddie continued to smile. After all, he was talking to her, and she thought he looked like a rock star. "Why?"

"Well, you know . . ." Nick found himself flustered under that steady gray stare. "Having a step-mother—a stepfamily."

"That's just a word." Gathering her nerve, she sat on the arm of the couch beside him. "We have a house in West Virginia—that's where Dad met Mama. He teaches at the university and she owns a toy store. Have you ever been to West Virginia?"

Nick was still stuck on her answer. *It's just a word.* He could hear in the easy tone of her voice that she meant just that. "What? Oh, no, never been there."

Inside the warm, fragrant kitchen, Rachel was laughing with her sister. "Katie certainly knows how to snag her man."

"It was sweet the way he blushed."

"Here." Nadia thrust a bowl into her eldest daughter's hands. "You make biscuits. The boy had good eyes," she said to Rachel. "Why is he in trouble?"

Sniffing a pot of simmering cabbage, Rachel smiled. "Because he didn't have a mama and papa to yell at him."

"And the older one," Nadia continued, opening the oven to check her ham. "He has good eyes, too. And they're on you."

"Maybe."

After smacking her daughter's hand away, Nadia replaced the lid on the pot. "Alex grumbles about them."

"He grumbles about everything."

Natasha cut shortening in the bowl and grinned. "I think it's more to the point that Rachel has her eye on Zack every bit as much as he has his on her."

"Thanks a lot," Rachel said under her breath.

"A woman who doesn't look at such a man needs glasses," Nadia said, and made her daughters laugh.

When her curiosity got to be too much for her, Rachel opened the swinging door a crack and peeked out. There was Sydney, sitting on the floor and keeping Brandon entertained with a pile of race cars. The men were huddled together, arguing football. Freddie was perched on the arm of the sofa, obviously in the first stages of infatuation with Nick. As for Nick, he seemed to have forgotten his embarrassment and was bouncing Katie on his knee. And Zack, she noted with a smile, was leaning forward, entrenched in the hot debate over the upcoming game.

By the time the table was set and groaning under the weight of platters of food, Zack was thoroughly fascinated with the Stanislaskis. They argued, loudly, but without any of the bitterness he remembered from his own confrontations with his father. He discovered that Mikhail was the artist who had crafted the sculpture on the piano, as well as all the passionate pieces in

Rachel's apartment. Yet he talked construction and building codes with his father, not art.

Natasha handled her children with a deft hand. No one seemed to mind if Brandon created a racket imitating race cars or if Katie climbed all over the furniture. But when it was time to stop, they did so at little more than a word from their mother or father.

Alex didn't seem like such a tough cop when he was being barraged by his family's teasing over his latest lady friend—a woman, Mikhail claimed, who had the I.Q. of the cabbage he was heaping on his plate.

"Hey, I don't mind. That way I can do the thinking for her."

That earned an unladylike snort from Rachel. "He wouldn't know how to handle a woman with a brain."

"One day one will find him," Nadia predicted. "Like Sydney found my Mikhail."

"She didn't find me." Mikhail passed a bowl of boiled potatoes to his wife. "I found her. She needed some spice in her life."

"As I recall, you needed someone to knock the chip off your shoulder."

"It was always so," Yuri agreed, shaking his fork. "He was a good boy, but— What is the word?"

"Arrogant?" Sydney suggested.

"Ah." Satisfied, Yuri dived into his meal. "But it's not so bad for a man to be arrogant."

"This is true." Nadia kept an eagle eye on Katie, who was concentrating on cutting her meat. "So long as he has a woman who is smarter. Is not hard to do."

Female laughter and male catcalls had Katie clapping her hands in delight.

"Nicholas," Nadia said, pleased that he was going back for seconds, "you will go to school, yes?"

"Ah...no, ma'am."

She urged the basket of biscuits on him. "So you know what work you want."

"I... Not exactly."

"He is young, Nadia," Yuri said from across the table. "Time to decide. You're skinny." He pursed his lips as he studied Nick. "But have good arms. You need work, I give you job. Teach you to build."

Speechless, Nick stared. No one had ever offered to give him anything so casually. The big, broad-faced man who was plowing through the glazed ham didn't even know him. "Thanks. But I'm sort of working for Zack."

"It must be interesting to work in a bar. Brandon, eat your vegetables, or no more biscuits. All the people you meet," Natasha continued, saving Katie's glass from tipping on the floor without breaking rhythm.

"You don't meet a whole lot of them in the kitchen," Nick muttered.

"You have to be twenty-one to tend bar or serve drinks," Zack reminded him.

Noting Nick's mutinous expression, Rachel broke in. "Mama, you should see Zack's cook. He's a giant from Jamaica, and he makes the most incredible food. I've been trying to charm some recipes out of him."

"I will give you one to trade."

"Make it the glaze for this ham, and I guarantee he'll give you anything." Zack sampled another bite. "It's great."

"You will take some home," Nadia ordered. "Make sandwiches."

"Yes, ma'am." Nick grinned.

Rachel bided her time, waiting until dinner was over and three of the four apple pies her mother had baked had been devoured. With just a little urging, Nadia was persuaded to play the piano. After a time, she and Spence played a duet, the music flowing out over the sound of clattering dishes and conversation.

She saw the way Nick glanced over, watching, listening. As cleverly as a general aligning his troops, she dropped down on the bench when Spence and Nadia took a break. She held out a hand, inviting Nick to join her.

"I shouldn't have had that second piece of pie," she said with a sigh.

"Me either." It was difficult to decide how to tell her the way the afternoon had made him feel. He wouldn't have believed people lived this way. "Your mom's great."

"Yeah, I think so." Very casually, she turned and began to noodle with the keys. "She and Papa love these Sundays when we can all get together."

"Your dad, he was saying how the house would get bigger when the kids left home. But now he thinks they'll have to add on a couple of rooms to hold everyone. I guess you get together like this a lot."

"Whenever we can."

"They didn't seem to mind you brought me and Zack along."

"They like company." She tried a chord, wincing at the clash of notes. "This always looks so easy when Spence or Mama does it."

"Try this." He put his hand over hers, guiding her fingers.

"Ah, better. But I don't see how anyone can play different things with each hand. At the same time, you know."

"You don't think about it that way. You just have to let it happen."

"Well..."

She trailed off and, unable to resist, he began to improvise blues. When the music moved through him, he forgot he was in a room crowded with people and let it take over. Even when the room fell silent, he continued, wrapped up in the pleasure of creating sound and feeling from the keys. When he played, he wasn't Nick LeBeck, outcast. He was someone he didn't really understand yet, someone he couldn't quite see and yearned desperately to be always.

He eased into half-remembered tunes, filling them out with his own interpretation, letting the music swing with his mood from blues to boogie-woogie to jazz and back again.

When he paused, grinning to himself from the sheer pleasure it had given him to play, Zack laid a hand on his shoulder and snapped him back to reality.

"Where'd you learn to do that?" The amazement in Zack's voice was reflected in his eyes. "I didn't know you could do that."

With a shrug, Nick wiped his suddenly nervous hands on his thighs. "I was just fooling around."

"That was some fooling around."

Cautious, trying to put a label on the tone of Zack's voice, Nick glanced back. "It's no big deal."

Grinning from ear to ear, Zack shook his head. "Man, to somebody who can't play 'Chopsticks,' that was one whale of a big deal." Pride was bubbling through the amazement. "It was great. Really great."

The pleasure working its way into him made Nick almost as uneasy as the criticism he'd expected. It was then he realized that everyone had stopped talking and was looking at him. Color crept into his cheeks. "Look, I said it was no big deal. I was just banging on the keys."

"That was some very talented banging." With Katie on his hip, Spencer moved to the piano. "Ever think about studying seriously?"

Flabbergasted, Nick stared down at his hands. It had been one thing to sit across the table from Spencer Kimball, and another entirely to have the renowned composer discussing music with him. "No... I mean, not really. I just fool around sometimes, that's all."

"You've got the touch, and the ear." Catching Rachel's eye, he passed her Katie and changed positions with her so that he sat with Nick on the edge of the piano bench. "Know any Muddy Waters?"

"Some. You dig Muddy Waters?"

"Sure." He began to play the bass. "Can you pick it up?"

"Yeah." Nick laid his hands on the keys and grinned. "Yeah."

"Not too shabby," Rachel murmured to Zack.

He was still staring at his brother, dumbfounded. "He never told me. Never a word." When Rachel reached for his hand, he gripped hard. "I guess he did to you."

"A little, enough to make me want to try this. I didn't know he was that good."

"He really is, isn't he?" Overwhelmed, he pressed his lips to Rachel's hair. Nick was too involved to notice, though several pair of eyes observed the gesture. "Looks like I'm going to have to get my hands on a piano."

Rachel leaned her head against his shoulder. "You're all right, Muldoon."

It took him nearly a week to arrange it, but taking another deep dip into his savings, Zack bought an upright piano. With Rachel's help, he dragged furniture around the apartment to make room for it.

Puffing a bit, her hands on her hips, she surveyed the space they had cleared under the window. "I wonder if it wouldn't be better against that wall there."

"You've already changed your mind three times. This is it." He took a long pull from a cold beer. "For better or worse."

"You're not marrying the stupid piano. You're arranging it. And I really think—"

"Keep thinking, and I'll pour this over your head." He caught her chin to tilt her head up for a kiss. "And it's not a stupid piano. The guy assured me it was the best for the money."

"Don't get started on that again." She eased closer to link her arms around his neck. "Nick doesn't need a baby grand."

"I'd just like to have done a little better for him."

"Muldoon." She pressed her mouth to his. "You did good. When's it supposed to get here?"

"Twenty minutes ago." Wound up, he began to pace. "If they blow this after I went through all that business to get Nick out for a few hours—"

Rachel interrupted him, amused and touched. "It's going to be fine. And I think it was inspired of you to use beer nuts to get him out of the way."

"He was steaming." With a grin, Zack dropped down on the couch. "Argued with me for ten minutes about why the hell he had to go check on a missing delivery of beer nuts when he was getting paid to wash dishes."

"I think he'll forgive you when he gets back."

"Hey up there." Rio's musical voice echoed up the stairway. "We got us one fine piano coming in. Best you come down and take a look."

Rachel tried to stay out of the way—though several times, as they muscled and maneuvered the piano up those steep stairs, she wanted to offer advice. The best part was watching Zack, which she did the entire time the instrument was hauled, set into place and tuned. He worried over the piano like a mother hen, wiping smudges from the surface, opening and closing the lid on the bench.

"That looks real fine." Rio folded his massive arms over his chest. "Be good to have music when I cook. You do right by that boy, Zack. He's going to make himself somebody. You'll see. Now I'm going to fix us something special." He grinned at Rachel. "When you going to bring that mama of yours by here so we can talk food?"

"Soon," Rachel promised. "She's going to bring you an old Ukrainian recipe."

"Good. Then I give her my secret barbecue sauce. I think she must be a fine woman." He started out just as Nick came clattering up the steps. "What's your hurry, boy? Got a fire in your pocket?"

"Damn beer nuts" was all Nick said as he pushed by. He swung into the apartment, ready for a fight. "Listen, bro, the next time you want somebody to—" Everything went out of his mind when he spotted the piano standing new and shiny under the window.

"Sorry about the wild-goose chase." Nervous, Zack jammed his hands in his pockets. "I wanted to get you out so we could get this in." He shifted back on his heels when Nick remained silent. "So, what do you think?"

Nick swallowed hard. "What did you do, rent it or something?"

"I bought it."

Because his fingers itched to feel the keys, he, too, stuck them in his pockets. Rachel nearly sighed. They looked like two stray dogs that didn't know whether to fight or make friends.

"You shouldn't have done that." The strain in Nick's voice made it come out curt and sharp.

"Why the hell not?" Zack shot back. His hands were now balled into fists and straining against denim. "It's my money. I thought it would be nice to have some music around here. So, do you want to try it out or not?"

There was an ache spreading, twisting in his gut and burning the back of his throat. He had to get out. "I forgot something," he muttered, and strode stiffly out the door.

"What the hell was that?" Zack exploded. He snatched up his beer, then set it down again before he gave in to the temptation to hurl the bottle against the wall. "If that little son of a—"

"Hold it." Rachel's order snapped out as she thumped a fist against Zack's chest. "Oh, the pair of you are a real prize. He doesn't know how to say thank you, and you're too stupid to see he was so overwhelmed he was practically on the verge of tears."

"That's bull. He all but tossed it back in my face."

"Idiot. You gave him a dream. It's very possibly the first time anyone ever understood what he wanted, deep down, and gave him a shot at it. He didn't know how to handle it, Zack, any more than you would."

"Listen, I—" He broke off and swore, because it made sense. "What am I supposed to do now?"

"Nothing." Cupping his face in her hands, she pulled it toward hers to kiss him. "Nothing at all. I'm going to go talk to him, okay?" She pulled back and started for the door.

"Rachel." He took a deep breath before crossing to her. "I need you." He watched surprise come into her eyes as he took her hands and brought them to his lips. "Maybe I don't know how to handle that, either."

Something fluttered around her heart. "You're doing all right, Muldoon."

"I don't think you understand." He didn't, either. "I really need you."

"I'm right here."

"But are you going to stay here, once your obligation to Nick is over?"

The fluttering increased. "We've got a couple of weeks before we have to think about that. It's..."

Steady, Rachel, she warned herself. Think it through. "It's not just Nick I care about." She tightened her fingers on his briefly before drawing away. "Let me go find him. We'll talk about the rest of this later."

"Okay." He stepped back from her, and from what he was feeling. "But I think we are going to have to talk about it. Soon."

With a quick nod, she hurried down the steps. Rio merely gestured toward the front of the bar, and, grateful she didn't have to talk for a moment, she went out to look.

She found him standing on the sidewalk with his hands balled in his pockets, staring at the late-afternoon traffic. Oh, she knew a portion of what he was feeling. How Zackary Muldoon could get inside you and pull your emotions apart before you had a chance to defend yourself.

Later, she promised herself, she would think about what he'd done to *her* emotions. For now, she would concentrate on Nick.

She stepped up beside him and brushed at the hair on his shoulders. "You doing okay?"

He didn't look at her, just continued to watch the fits and starts of traffic. "Why did he do that?"

"Why do you think?"

"I didn't ask him for anything."

"The best gifts are the ones we don't ask for."

He shifted, meeting her eyes for the barest of moments. "Did you talk him into it?"

"No." Trying to be patient, she took him by the arms so that he had to face her. "Open your eyes, Nick. You saw the way he reacted when he heard you play. He was so proud of you he could barely talk. He wanted to give you something that would matter to you. He didn't do it so you'd be obligated to him, but because he loves you. That's what families do.''

"Your family."

She gave him a quick shake. "And yours. Don't try to con me with that bull about not being real brothers. You care just as much about him as he does about you. I know how much it meant to you to walk in there and see that piano. Mama had the same look on her face on Mother's Day, but it was easier for her to show what she was feeling. You just need a little practice."

Closing his eyes, he laid his brow against hers. "I don't know what to say to him. How to act. Nobody's ever . . . I've never had anybody. When I was a kid, I just wanted to hang around him. Then he took off."

"I know. Try to remember he wasn't much more than a kid himself when he did. He's not going anywhere now." Rachel kissed both his cheeks, as her mother might have done. "Why don't you go back inside, Nick, and do what you do best?"

"What's that?"

She smiled at him. "Play it by ear. Go on. He's dying for you to try it out."

"Yeah. Okay." He took a step back. "You coming?"

"No, I've got some things to do." Some things to think about, she thought, correcting herself. "Tell Zack I'll see him later."

But she waited after he'd gone in. Standing on the sidewalk, she watched the window. And after a while, very faintly, she heard the sound of music.

Chapter Ten

"Yo, Rachel." Pete straightened on his stool and sucked in some of his comfortable stomach when he spotted Rachel swinging through the front door of the bar. "How 'bout I buy you a drink?"

"I might just let you do that." But her smile was for Zack as she hung her coat on one of the hooks by the door. As she crossed the room, she shot a meaningful glance at the blonde who was seductively wrapped around a bar stool, purring an order for another drink while she walked her fingers up Zack's arm. "Busy night?"

Lola juggled a tray as she passed. "That one's on her third stinger," she said to Rachel under her breath. "And those big blue eyes of hers have been crawling all over the boss for two hours."

"That's all she'll do—unless she wants those eyes black-and-blue."

Lola gave a snap of appreciative laughter. "Atta girl. Hey, hold on a minute." With a skill Rachel admired, Lola served a full tray of drinks, emptied ashtrays and replaced an empty basket of chips. "See the brunette by the juke?"

With her lips pursed, Rachel studied the slim jean-clad hips and the waterfall of honey-brown hair. "Don't tell me I have to worry about her, too?"

"No, *I* do. That's my oldest."

"Your daughter? She's gorgeous."

"Yeah. That's why I have to worry. Anyway, Zack's been hinting around about how he'd like Nick to meet some people closer to his own age, so I talked her into coming in, having one of Rio's burgers."

"And?"

"Nick looked. Actually, he was pretty enthusiastic about busing tables tonight. But he didn't make a move in her direction."

"Looking's good," Rachel mused. "It wouldn't bother you if he was interested enough to ask her out?"

"Nick's okay. Besides, my Terri can take care of herself." Lola winked. "Takes after her mom. Keep your pants on," she shouted to the table of four that was signaling to her. "Catch you later."

"Well, now..." Rachel eased onto the stool between Harry and Pete. A glass of white wine was already waiting for her. "What's the latest?"

"Seven-letter word for rapture," Harry told her. "Ending in 'y'."

Rachel smiled into her wine. *"Ecstasy,"* she said, watching Zack.

"Okay!" Pleased with that, he skimmed over the blank spaces in his puzzle. "Here's another seven. Characterized by a lack of substance."

"Perfect," she murmured, shifting her gaze to the blonde, who was leaning her cleavage over the bar. "Try *vacuous.*"

"Damn, you're good."

"Harry," she gave him a smile that had him going beet red, "I'm terrific. Keep an eye on things for me. I want to talk to Nick."

Pete watched her go, sighed. "If I was twenty years younger, thirty pounds lighter, didn't have a wife who'd slit my wrists and still had all my hair..."

"Yeah. Keep dreaming." Harry signaled for another round.

The minute she passed into the kitchen, Rachel took a deep breath. It always smelled like heaven. "Okay, Rio, what's good tonight?"

"Everything's always good." He grinned, wiping his big hands on his apron. "But tonight my fried chicken's number one."

"There must be a drumstick with my name on it. Hey, Nick." Now as at home here as she was in her mama's kitchen, she eased against the counter where he was stacking the dishes. "How's it going?"

"By last count, I've washed six thousand and eighty-two plates." But he smiled when he said it. "Zack mentioned you might be coming by tonight. I've been looking for you."

Rio handed her a plate heaped with fried chicken, creamed potatoes and coleslaw. "If I came by any more often, they'd have to roll me in and out the door."

"You eat." Rio gestured with his spatula before he flipped burgers. "I like to see a woman with hips."

"You're about to." Her willpower was nonexistent when she was faced with Rio's extra-spicy chicken. Rachel began to eat where she stood. "Definitely number one," she said with her mouth full. Rio grinned. "So, did you want to see me about anything in particular?" she asked Nick.

"No." He brushed a hand down her hair. "I just wanted to see you."

Whoops. "Nick, I really think—"

"We've only got a couple of weeks to go."

"I know." She shifted slightly, putting the plate between them. "In fact, I was able to speak to the DA, tell him about your progress. He doesn't plan on making an objection to the suspended sentence and probation we expect from Judge Beckett."

"I knew I could count on you, but I wasn't just thinking about that."

She knew very well what he was thinking of, and she'd put off dealing with it long enough. "Rio—" she set the plate aside "—I need to talk to Nick for a minute. Can you handle things without him if we go upstairs?"

"No problem. He just wash twice as fast when he come back."

She would be calm, Rachel promised herself as they started upstairs. She would be logical, and she would be in control. "Okay, Nick," she said the minute they stepped into the apartment. And that was all she said, because she found herself being thoroughly kissed. "Stop." Her voice was muffled, but it was firm, and the hands she shoved against his shoulders did the rest.

"I've missed you, that's all." He gentled his grip, then released her completely when she stepped back. "It's been a long time since we had a chance to be alone."

Pressing her hands to her temples, she sighed. "Oh, Nick. I've made a mess of this." The confused churning of emotion was clear in her eyes as she stared at him. "I kept telling myself it would resolve itself, even though I knew it wouldn't." In a gesture that mirrored the helplessness she was feeling, she let her hands drop to her sides. "I don't want to hurt you."

There was a quick warning twist in his gut. People only said that stuff about not hurting you in that particular tone of voice when they were about to. "What are you talking about?"

"About you and me—about you thinking there's a you and me." She turned away, hoping she could find the right words. "I tried to explain it to you before, but I did a poor job of it. You see, initially I was so surprised that you would think of me that way. I didn't—" With a sound of disgust, she turned to face him again. "I'm not handling it any better now."

"Why don't you just say what you mean?"

"I care about you, not only as my client, but as a person."

That all-too-familiar light came into his eyes. "I care about you, too."

When he took a step toward her, she lifted her hands, palms out. "But not that way, Nick. Not...romantically."

His eyes narrowed, and she watched, hurting, as he absorbed the rejection. "You're not interested in me."

"I am interested in you, but not the way you think you'd like me to be."

"I get the picture." Trying to tough it out, he hooked his thumbs in his front pockets. "You think I'm too young."

She thought about the way she'd just been kissed, and let out a long breath. "That argument doesn't seem altogether valid. It should, but you're not a typical teenager."

"So what is it? I'm just not your type?"

When she thought of how much he and Zack had in common, she had to block a quick laugh. "That doesn't work either." Sorry that she was going to hurt him, knowing she had to, Rachel did her best with the truth. "What I feel for you is the same sort of thing I feel for my brothers. I'm sorry it's not what you want, Nick, but it's all I can give." She wanted to reach out, touch his arm, but she was afraid he'd shrug her off. "I'm sorry, too, that I didn't put it just that way weeks ago. I didn't seem to know how."

"I feel like an idiot."

"Don't." She couldn't keep herself from reaching out now, taking his hand in hers. "There's nothing for you to feel like an idiot about. You were attracted, and you were honest about it. And underneath all my confusion and dismay," she added, trying out a smile, "I was very flattered."

"I'd rather you said you were tempted."

"Maybe." Her smile warmed, squeezing his battered heart. "For a moment. I hope it doesn't hurt you to have me say it, but I do want to be your friend."

"Well, you gave it to me straight." And he supposed he would have to accept it. A babe was just a babe, he tried to tell himself. But he knew there was no one else like Rachel. "No hard feelings."

"Good." She wanted to kiss him, but figured it was best not to push her luck. Or his. She did take his other hand. "I always wanted a younger brother."

He wasn't quite ready to take that position. "Why?"

"For the purest of reasons," she told him. "To have somebody I could push around." When he smiled, she felt the first genuine tug of relief. "Come on, get back to work."

She walked down with him, certain they had progressed to the next stage. To reassure herself, she stayed in the kitchen for a few minutes, pleased when she felt no lingering tension from Nick's direction.

When she slipped out, she looked immediately for Zack.

"In the office," Pete told her, grinning. "You should go right on in."

"Thanks." She was puzzled by the chuckles that rumbled around the bar, but when she glanced back, everyone looked busy and innocent. Too innocent, Rachel thought as she pushed open Zack's office door.

He was there all right, big as life, standing in front of his shipshape desk. There was a curvy blonde wrapped around him, clinging like cellophane.

With one brow arched, Rachel took in the scene. The blonde was doing her best to crawl up Zack's body. She nearly had him pinned to the desk, and Zack was tugging at the arms that roped his neck. The expression on his face, Rachel mused—a kind of baffled embarrassment—was worth the price of admission all by itself.

"Listen, honey, I appreciate the offer. Really. But I'm not—" He broke off when he spotted Rachel.

That expression, she decided, was even better. This one had traces of shock, chagrin and apology, all seasoned with a nice dollop of fear.

"Oh, God." He managed to pry one arm from around his neck, and he tried to shake her off, but she transferred her grip to his waist.

"Excuse me," Rachel said, her tongue firmly in her cheek. "I can see you're busy."

"Damn it, don't shut the door." His eyes widened when the blonde shifted to give his bottom a nice, intimate squeeze. "Give me a break, Rachel."

"You want a break?" She glanced back to where the regulars had moved closer, craning their necks to catch the show. "He wants a break," she told them. Very casually, she strolled across the threshold. "Which leg would you like me to break, Muldoon? Or would you prefer an arm? Maybe your neck."

"Have a heart." The blonde was giggling now as she tugged at his sweater. "Help me get her off. She's plowed."

"I'd think a big strong man like you could handle that all by yourself."

"She moves like a damn eel," he muttered. "Come on, Babs, let go. I'll call you a cab."

She was slithering over him, Rachel noted, and with a sigh she took charge. Gripping the blonde's artfully tangled mane in one hand, she tugged. Hard. The quick squeal of pain was very satisfying. Following up on it, Rachel shoved her face close. "You're trespassing, dear."

Babs weaved, gave a glazed-eyed grin. "I didn't see any signs."

"Consider yourself lucky I don't make you see stars." Using the hair as a leash, Rachel pulled the squeaking blonde to the door. "This way out."

"I'll take it from here." Lola slipped an arm around the blonde's waist. "Come on, sweetie, you're looking a little green."

"He's just so damn cute," Babs sighed as she stumbled toward the ladies' room with Lola.

"Call her a cab," Zack shouted. After one heated glare at the grinning faces of his customers, he slammed the door shut. "Listen, Rachel..." Besides being mortified, he was out of breath, and he took a moment to steady himself. "It wasn't the way it looked."

"Oh?" The situation was too entertaining to resist. She sauntered over to his desk, scooted onto the edge and crossed her legs. "How did it look, Muldoon?"

"You know damn well." He blew out a breath, tucked his useless hands in his pockets. "She got herself wasted on a couple of stingers. I came in to call her a cab, and she followed me." His brows drew together when Rachel lifted a hand to examine her nails. "She attacked me."

"Want to press charges?"

"Don't get cute with me." As embarrassing moments went, Zack considered this in the top ten. "I was trying to... defend myself."

"I could see it was a pitched battle. You're lucky you came out of it alive."

"What was I supposed to do, knock her cold?" He paced from one wall to the other. "I told her I wasn't interested, but she wouldn't back off."

"You're just so damn cute," Rachel said, fluttering her lashes.

"Funny," he tossed over his shoulder. "Really funny. You're going to play this one out all the way, aren't you?"

"Bingo." She picked up a letter opener from his desk, tested the point, thoughtfully. "As counsel for the defense, I have to ask if you feel that strutting behind the bar in those snug black jeans—"

"I don't strut."

"I'll rephrase the question." She flicked the tip of the letter opener with her thumb. "Can you say—and I remind you, Mr. Muldoon, you're under oath—can you tell this court you haven't done anything to entice the defendant, to make her believe you were available? Even willing?"

"I never... Well, I might have before you..." As a man of the sea, Zack knew when to cut line. He crossed his arms over his chest. "I take the Fifth."

"Coward."

"You bet." He eyed the letter opener warily. "You don't plan to use that on any particularly sensitive part of my anatomy?"

Letting her gaze skim down, Rachel touched her tongue to her upper lip. "Probably not."

His smile came slowly and was full of relief. "You're really not mad, are you, sugar?"

"That I walked in and found you in a compromising position with a blond bombshell?" After a quick laugh, she shifted her grip on the letter opener. "Why should I be mad, sugar?"

"You may have saved my life." He thought he'd gauged her mood correctly, but his approach was still cautious. "You don't know what she said she was going to do to me." He gave a mock shudder, and slipped his arms around her, as if for support. "She's a yoga instructor."

"Oh, my." Biting back a grin, Rachel patted his back. "What did she threaten you with?"

"Well, I think it went something like..." He leaned close to her ear, whispering. He heard Rachel's surprised chuckle. "And then..."

"Oh, *my*" was all she could say. She swallowed once. "Do you think that's anatomically possible?"

"I think you'd have to be double-jointed, but we could give it a try."

Wicked laughter gleaming in her eyes, she tilted her head back. "I don't care what you say, Muldoon. I think you liked being pawed."

"Uh-uh." He nuzzled her neck. "It was degrading. I feel so... cheap."

"There, there. I saved you."

"You were a regular Viking."

"And you know what they say about Vikings..." she murmured as she turned her mouth to his.

"Go ahead," he said invitingly. "Use me."

"Oh, I plan to."

The kiss was long and satisfying, but as it began to heat he tore his mouth from hers to bury his face in her hair.

"Rachel, you don't know how good you feel. How right."

"I know this feels right." Eyes shut tightly, she held him close.

"Do you?"

"Yes. I think..." She let her words trail off into a sigh. She'd been doing a great deal of thinking over the past few days. "I think sometimes people just fit. The way you told me once before."

He drew back, cupping her face in his hands. His eyes were very dark, very intense, on hers. She wasn't entirely sure what she was reading in them, but it made her heart trip-hammer into her throat. "We fit. I know you said you didn't want to get involved. That you have priorities."

She linked her fingers around his wrists. "I said a lot of things."

"Rachel, I want you to move in with me." He saw the surprise in her eyes and hurried on before she could answer. "I know you wanted to keep it simple. So did I. This doesn't have to be a complication. You'd have time to think about it. We have to wait until everything's straightened out with Nick. But I need for you to know how much I want to be with you—not just snatching time."

She let out an unsteady breath. "It's a big step."

"And you don't do things on impulse." He lowered his lips to brush hers. "Think about it. Think about this," he whispered, and took the kiss deep, deep, fathoms deep, until thinking was impossible.

"Zack, I need to—" Nick burst into the office, and froze. He saw Rachel pressed against his brother, her hands fisted in his hair, her eyes soft and clouded.

They cleared quickly enough, and now there was alarm there, and apology. But as Nick stared at them, all he could see was the red mist of betrayal.

She shouted his name as Nick leaped. Zack saw the blow coming, and he let it connect. It rocked him back on his heels. He tasted blood. Instinct had him gripping Nick's wrists to prevent another punch, but Nick twisted away, agile as a snake, and braced for the next round.

"Stop it!" Heedless that the next fist could fly any second, Rachel stepped furiously between them, shoving them apart. "This isn't the way."

Clamping down on his own temper, Zack merely lifted her up and set her aside. "Stay clear. You want to go a round in here?" he said to Nick. "Or take it outside?"

"Of all the—"

"Anywhere you say," Nick snapped, cutting Rachel off. "You son of a bitch. It was always you." He shoved, but the bright hurt in his eyes kept Zack from striking back. "You always had to come out on top, didn't you?" His breathing was labored as he rammed Zack back against the wall. "All this crap about family. Well, you know where you can stick it, *bro.*"

"Nick, please." Rachel lifted a hand, but let it drop when he turned those furious eyes on her.

"Just shut up. That whole line of bull you handed me upstairs. You've got real talent, lady, because I was buying it. You knew how I felt, and all the time you're making it with him behind my back."

"Nick, it wasn't like that."

"You lying bitch."

His head snapped back when Zack clipped him with a backhand. There was blood on both sides now. "You want to take a swing at me, go ahead. But you don't talk to her like that."

Teeth gritted, Nick wiped the blood from his lip. He wanted to hate. Needed to. "The hell with you. The hell with both of you."

He swung on his heel and darted out.

"Oh, God." Rachel covered her face, but it did nothing to erase the image of the hurt she'd seen in

Nick's eyes. The damage, she thought miserably, that she had done. "What a mess. I'm going after him."

"Leave him alone."

"It's my fault," she said, dropping her arms to her sides. "I have to try."

"I said leave him alone."

"Damn it, Zack—"

"Excuse me." There was a rap on the door, which Nick had left hanging open. Rachel turned and bit back a groan.

"Judge Beckett."

"Good evening, Ms. Stanislaski. Mr. Muldoon, I dropped in for one of your famous manhattans. Perhaps you could mix one for me while I have a conference with your brother's attorney."

"Your Honor," Rachel began, "my client..."

"I saw your client as he roared out of here. Your mouth's bleeding, Mr. Muldoon." She turned and shot a look at Rachel. "Counselor?"

"Perfect timing," Rachel said under her breath. "I'll handle this," she said to Zack. "Don't worry. And once Nick works off a little steam—"

"He'll come back smiling?" Zack finished. His temper was fading, but guilt was moving full steam ahead. "I don't think so. And it's not your fault." He wished he had more than his own empty sense of failure to give her. "He's my brother. I'm responsible." He shook his head before she could speak. "Let me go fix the judge her drink."

He brushed by her. Rachel reached out to stop him, then let her hand fall away. There was nothing she could say to ease the hurt. But she had a chance to minimize the damage with Judge Beckett.

She found the judge looking attractive and relaxed at a table on the far side of the bar. Yet the aura of power the woman had when wearing black robes on the bench wasn't diminished in the least by the trim blue slacks and white sweater she wore tonight.

"Have a seat, Counselor."

"Thank you."

Beckett smiled, tapping rose-tipped nails on the edge of the table. "I can see the wheels turning. How much do I tell her, how much do I evade? I always enjoy having you in my courtroom, Ms. Stanislaski. You have style."

"Thank you," Rachel said again. Their drinks arrived, and she took the time while they were served to gather her thoughts. "I'm afraid you might, understandably, misinterpret what you saw tonight, Your Honor."

"Are you?" With a smile, Beckett sampled her drink. She shifted her gaze to meet Zack's and sent him an approving smile. "And what would you consider my interpretation?"

"Obviously, Nick and his brother were arguing."

"Fighting," Beckett corrected, stirring the cherry around in her drink before biting it from its stem. "Arguing involves words. And, while words may leave scars, they don't draw blood."

"You don't have brothers, do you, Your Honor?"

"No, I don't."

"I do."

With a lift of a brow, Beckett sipped again. "All right, I'll sustain that. What were they arguing about?"

Rachel eased around the boggy ground. "It was just a misunderstanding. I won't deny both of them are hotheaded, and that with their type of temperament a misunderstanding can sometimes evolve into..."

"An argument?" Beckett suggested.

"Yes." Needing to make her point, Rachel leaned forward. "Judge Beckett, Nick has been making such incredible progress. When I was first assigned to his case, I very nearly dismissed him as just another street punk. But there was something that made me reevaluate him."

"Haunted eyes do that to a woman."

Surprised, Rachel blinked. "Yes."

"Go on."

"He was so young, and yet he'd already started to give up on himself, and everyone else. After I met Zack, and found out about Nick's background, it was easy to understand. There's never been anyone permanent in his life, anyone he felt he could count on and trust. But with Zack... he wanted to. No matter how tough and disinterested he tried to act, the longer he was with Zack, the more you could see that they needed each other."

"Just how involved are you with your co-guardian?"

With her face carefully blank, Rachel sat back in her seat. "I believe that's irrelevant."

"Do you? Well." She gestured with her hand. "Continue."

"For nearly two months, Nick has stayed out of trouble. He's been handling the responsibilities Zack has given him. He's developing outside interests. He plays the piano."

"Does he?"

"Zack bought him one when he found out."

"That doesn't seem like something that would make fists fly." A faint smile played around her mouth as she gestured with her manhattan. "You're dodging the point, Counselor."

"I want you to understand that this probationary period has been successful. What happened tonight was simply a product of misunderstandings and hot tempers. It was the exception rather than the rule."

"You're not in court."

"No, Your Honor, but I don't want you to hold this against my client when I am."

"Agreed." Pleased with what she saw in Rachel, what she heard, and what she sensed, Beckett rattled the ice in her glass. "Explain tonight."

"It was my fault," Rachel said, pushing her wine aside. "It was poor judgment on my part that caused Nick to feel, to believe he felt . . . something."

Beckett pursed her lips. "I begin to see. He's a healthy young man, and you're an attractive woman who's shown an interest in him."

"And I blew it," Rachel said bitterly. "I thought I'd handled it. I was so damn sure I was on top of everything."

"I know the feeling." Beckett sampled a beer nut thoughtfully. "Off the record. Start at the beginning."

Hoping her own culpability would lighten Nick's load, even if it got her thrown off the case, Rachel explained. Beckett said nothing, only nodding or making interested noises now and again. "And when he walked into the office and saw Zack and me together," she concluded, "all he saw was betrayal. I know I had no right to become involved with Zack. Excuses don't cut it."

"Rachel, you're an excellent attorney. That doesn't preclude your having a private life."

"When it endangers my relationship with a client—"

"Don't interrupt. I'll grant that you may have exercised poor judgment in this instance. I'll also grant that one can't always choose the time, place or circumstances for falling in love."

"I didn't say I was in love."

Beckett smiled. "I noticed that. It's easier to beat yourself up about it if you tell yourself love had nothing to do with it." Her smile widened. "No rebuttal, Counselor? Just as well, because I haven't finished. I could tell you you've lost your objectivity, but you already know that. I, for one, am not entirely sure objectivity is always the answer. There are so many shades between right and wrong. Finding the one that fits is something we struggle with every day. Your client is trying to find his. You may not be able to help."

"I don't want to let him down."

"Better you should do what's possible to prevent him from letting himself down. Sometimes it works, sometimes it doesn't. You'll discover how often it doesn't when it's your turn to sit on the bench."

The understanding in Beckett's eyes had Rachel reaching for her wine again. "I didn't know I was that transparent."

"Oh, to one who's been there, certainly." Amused, Beckett tapped her glass against Rachel's. "A few more years of seasoning, Counselor, and you'll make quite a competent judge. That *is* what you want?"

"Yes." She met Beckett's eyes levelly. "That's exactly what I want."

"Good. Now, since I've had a drink and I'm feeling rather mellow, I'll tell you something—off the record. It was almost thirty years ago that I was you. So very close to who and what you are. Things were more difficult for women in our position than they are now. They're far from perfect now," she added, setting her glass aside, "but some of the battles are over. I had to make choices. Those professional-versus-personal choices that men rarely have to make. Do I have a family or do I have a career? I don't regret choosing my career."

She glanced back at the bar, at Zack, and sighed. "Or only rarely. But times change, and even a professionally ambitious woman doesn't have to make an either-or decision. She can have both, if she's clever. You strike me as a clever woman."

"I like to think so," Rachel murmured. "But it doesn't make it any less terrifying."

"That kind of terror makes life worthwhile. I don't think nerves will stop you, Counselor. I don't think anything will. In the meantime, see that you and your client are prepared for the hearing."

When Beckett rose, Rachel was instantly on her feet. "Judge Beckett, about tonight—"

"I came in for a drink. It's a nice bar. Clean, friendly. As for my decision, that will depend on what I see and hear in my courtroom. Understood?"

"Yes. Thank you."

"Tell Mr. Muldoon he makes an excellent manhattan."

With her emotions still in a state of upheaval, Rachel watched Beckett stroll out.

"How bad is it?" Zack asked from behind her.

Rachel merely shook her head, reaching back to take his hand. "She likes the way you mix a drink." Turning to him, she comforted him with a hug. "And I think I've just met another intelligent woman with a weakness for bad boys. It's going to be all right."

"If Nick doesn't come back..."

"He'll be back." She needed to believe it. Needed to make Zack believe it. "He's mad, and he's hurt, but he's not stupid." She gave his hand another quick squeeze and smiled up at him. "He's too much like you."

"I shouldn't have hit him."

"Intellectually, I agree. Emotionally..." Because passion was a part of her life, she shrugged it off. "I've seen my brothers pound on each other too often to believe it's the end of the world. I've got to go." She touched a gentle kiss to his swollen lip. "When he comes back, it's probably best if I'm not here. But I want you to call me when he shows up, no matter what time it is."

"I don't like you going home alone," he said as he walked with her to where her coat was hanging.

"I'll take a cab." The fact that he didn't argue made her realize just how distracted he was. "We're going to work this out, Zack. Trust me."

"Yeah. I'll call you."

She stepped outside and headed down to the corner to hail a cab. Trust me, she'd told him. She could only hope she deserved that trust.

Chapter Eleven

She nearly called Alex when she got home, but she was afraid that if her brother put out feelers, even unofficially, Nick would only be more furious.

All she could do was wait. And wait alone.

An odd triangle they made, she thought as she wandered restlessly around her apartment with a rapidly cooling cup of tea. Nick, young and defiant, seeing rejection and betrayal everywhere, even as he looked so desperately for his place in the world. And Zack, so innately generous, so fueled by passion and so vulnerable to his brother. And herself, the objective, logical and ambitious attorney who'd fallen in love with them both.

Maybe she should be writing soap operas, she thought as she dropped down on the couch. She curled up her legs, cupping her mug in both hands. If she had the imagination for that, at least she might be able to write herself out of this situation.

Oh, how had it happened? she wondered, and closed her tired eyes. She was the one who had had things aligned so clearly. Hadn't she always known exactly where she was going and how she was going to get there? Every obstacle that could possibly block her path had been considered and weighed. All the options, all the ways of going around or through those obstacles, had been calculated.

All of them.

Except Zackary Muldoon.

By becoming involved with him, by letting her emotions rule her head, she'd made a mess of everything. It was entirely possible that Nick, pumped by hurt and frustration, would race headlong into trouble before the night was over. However understanding and compassionate Judge Beckett was, if Nick broke his probation, she would have no choice but to sentence him.

Even if the sentence was light, how could she forgive herself? How could Zack forgive her for failing? And, worst of all, how could Nick rebound from that final rejection when society put him behind bars?

She wanted to believe he'd go back to Zack. Angry, yes...defiant, certainly...maybe even spoiling for a fight. All those things could be dealt with, if only he went back.

But if he didn't...

The sound of her buzzer had her jolting. Well aware that it was after midnight, she unfolded herself, hoping it was Zack coming by to tell her Nick was safe and sound.

"Yes?"

"I want to come up." It was Nick's voice, edgy and demanding. Rachel had to bite back a cry of relief.

"Sure." She kept her tone light as she released the lock. "Come ahead."

She pressed her fingers against her eyes to push back the tears that filled them. It was stupid to get so emotional. Hadn't logic told her he'd have to come back? Hadn't she said as much to Zack?

But when the knock rapped sharply at her door, she was swinging it open, and the words were tumbling out. "I was so worried. I was going to go after you, but I didn't know where to start to look. Oh, Nick, I'm sorry. I'm so sorry."

"Sorry it blew up in your face?" He shoved the door closed behind him. He hadn't intended to come here, but he'd been walking, walking. Then it had seemed like the only place to go. "Sorry I came in and found you with Zack?"

It was far from over, Rachel realized. What she saw in his eyes was just as dangerous as what had been in them when he'd leaped across the office at Zack. "I'm sorry I hurt you."

"You're sorry I found out what you really are. You're nothing but a liar."

"I never lied to you."

"Every time you opened your mouth." He hadn't moved away from the door, and his hands were balled into fists, white-knuckled, at his side. "You and Zack. The whole time you were pretending to care about me, acting as if you liked being with me, you were making it with him."

"I do care—" she began, but he cut her off.

"I can see what a kick the two of you must've gotten out of it. Poor, pathetic Nick, mooning around, trying to make something of himself because he had a case on the sexy lawyer. I guess the two of you lay in bed and laughed yourself sick.''

"No. It was never like that."

"Are you going to tell me you didn't go to bed with him?"

He saw the truth in her eyes before her own temper kicked in. "You're out of line. I'm not going to discuss—"

His hands shot out, snatching the lapels of her robe and swinging her around. Her back rammed hard into the door. The first bubble of fear evaporated in her throat as Nick pushed his face close to hers. All she could see was his eyes, sharp green and glinting with fury.

"Why did you do it? Why did you have to make a fool out of me? Why did it have to be my brother?"

"Nick." She had his wrists now, and she tried to drag them away. But rage had added weight to his sinewy strength.

"Do you know how it makes me feel to know that while I was imagining us you were with him? And he knew. He knew."

Her breath was hitching, but she fought to control it. "You're hurting me."

She thought the statement would come out calm, even authoritative. Instead, it was shaky, and the fear underneath it clear even in his reckless state. His eyes went blank for a moment, then focused on his hands. They were digging into her shoulders. Appalled, he pulled them away and stared at her.

"I'm going."

Sometimes all you had was impulse. Rachel went with it and pressed her back against the door. "Don't. Please. Don't go like this."

There was a churning in his stomach that was pure self-loathing. "I never pushed a woman around before. It's as low as it gets."

"You didn't hurt me. I'm okay."

What she was, he noted, was deathly pale. "You're shaking."

"Okay, I'm shaking. Can we sit down?"

"I shouldn't have come here, Rachel. I shouldn't have jumped on you that way."

"I'm glad you came. Let's leave it at that for a minute. Please, let's sit down."

Because he was afraid she'd stay pressed against the door trembling until he agreed, he nodded. "You've got some things to toss back at me. I figure I owe you that." As he sat, his shoulders slumped. "I guess you'll ask to be taken off the case."

"That has nothing to do with this. But no." She thought about picking up her cold tea, but she was afraid her hands weren't steady enough. "This is personal, Nick. I'm the one who screwed up by blurring the lines. I knew better. There's no excuse." Inhaling deeply, she linked her fingers in her lap. "What happened between Zack and me wasn't planned, and it certainly wasn't professional."

He gave a quick snort. "Now you're going to tell me you couldn't help yourself."

"No," she said quietly. "I could have. There's always a choice. I didn't want to help myself."

Her answer, and the tone of it, had him frowning. He'd been certain she would try to find an easy way out. "So, you chose him."

"What happened was immediate, and maybe a little overwhelming..." She wasn't certain there were words to describe what had happened between her and Zack. "In any case, I could have stopped it. Or at least postponed it. I didn't, and that fault lies with me. The fact that we were both your guardians made it a poor call, but—" She shook her head. "No buts. It was a poor call." Her eyes met his, pleaded for trust. "We never thought of you as poor or pathetic. We never laughed at you. Whatever you think of me, don't let it ruin what you've started to get back with Zack."

"He moved in on me."

"Nick." Her voice held both patience and compassion. "He didn't. You know he didn't."

He did know, wondered if he had always known, that his relationship with Rachel had never been anything more than a fantasy. But knowing it didn't ease the raw wounds of rejection.

"I cared about you."

"I know." Her eyes filled again, and spilled over before she could prevent it. "I'm sorry."

"God, Rachel. Don't." He didn't think he could stand it. First he'd terrified her, and now he was making her cry. "Don't do that."

"I won't." But as quickly as she swiped at the tears, more fell. "I just feel so lousy about it all. When I look back, I can see a dozen ways I should've handled things. I'm usually in control." Her breath hitched as she fought for composure. "I hate, I really hate, that I've come between the two of you."

"Hey, come on." He was totally at a loss. When he rose to cross to her, he was surprised he didn't leave a trail of slime on her rug. "Listen, take it easy, okay?"

He patted her shoulder awkwardly. "I've been dumped before."

All that did was force her to fumble in the pocket of her robe for a tissue. "Don't hate him because of this."

"Don't ask for miracles."

"Oh, Nick, if you could only see through all the mistakes to what you mean to him."

"No lectures." Since her tears seemed to be drying up, he felt he could take a stand on that. "You carry on like you're in love with him." He was stunned when he saw the look in her eyes, the miserable, heartsick look, before they filled again. "Oh, man." While she crumpled into sobs, he readjusted his thinking. "You mean it's not just sex?"

"It was supposed to be." His arm went around her tentatively, and she leaned into it. "Oh, God, how did I get into all this? I don't want to be in love with anybody."

"That's rough." It occurred to Nick that he was holding her close but there weren't any tingles or tugs. The hell of it was, he was feeling almost brotherly. No one had ever cried on his shoulder before, or looked to him for support. "How about him? Is he stuck in the same groove?"

"I don't know." She sniffled, blew her nose. "We haven't talked about it. We aren't going to talk about it. The whole thing's ridiculous. I'm ridiculous." Thoroughly ashamed, she eased back. "Let's just say it's been an emotional night all around. Please, don't say anything to him about this."

"I figure that's up to you."

"Good. I appreciate it." Still shaky, she wiped at a stray tear with the back of her hand. "Don't hate me too much."

"I don't hate you." He leaned back, suddenly exhausted. "I don't know what I feel. Maybe I thought I could come up here tonight and prove to you I was the better man. Pretty stupid."

"You're both pretty special," she told him. "Why else would a nice, sensible woman like me fall for both of you?"

He turned his head to give her a weak smile. "You sure can pick 'em."

"Yeah." She touched his cheek. "I sure can. Tell me you're going back."

His lips flattened. "Where else would I go?"

That didn't satisfy her. "Tell me you're going back to talk things through with him, to work things out."

"I can't tell you that."

When he started to stand, she took his hand. "Let me go back with you. I want to help. I need to feel as though I've made some of this up to the two of you."

"You didn't do anything but fall for the wrong guy."

She took a great deal of comfort from the familiar smirk. "You may be right. Let me come anyway."

"Suit yourself. You might want to wash your face. Your eyes are red."

"Great. Give me five minutes."

Rachel could feel Nick start to tense up half a block from Lower the Boom. His shoulders were hunched, his brows were lowered, his hands were jammed in his pockets.

Typical, she thought. The male animal ruffles his fur and bares his teeth to show the opposing male how tough he is.

She kept the observation to herself, knowing neither of these males would appreciate it.

"Here's the idea," she said, pausing by the door. "It was a pretty slow night, and it's already after one. We'll wait until the bar closes, and you two can say your piece. I'll be mediator."

Nick wondered if she had any idea how hard it was for him to face what was on the other side of that door. "Whatever."

"And if there are any punches thrown," she added as she pulled the door open, "I'll throw them."

That brought the ghost of a smile to his face. It faded as soon as they stepped in.

Rachel had been right. It was a slow night, as it often was in the middle of the week. Most of the regulars had already headed off to home and hearth. A few diehards lingered at the bar, which Zack was manning alone. Lola was busy wiping down the tables. She glanced up, shot Rachel a satisfied look, then went back to work.

Zack took a pull from a bottle of mineral water. Rachel saw his eyes change, recognized the relief in them before the shutters came down.

"Hey, barkeep—" Rachel slid onto a stool "—got any coffee?"

"Sure."

"Make it two," she said, sending a meaningful glance in Nick's direction.

He said nothing, but he did sit beside her.

"There's an old Ukrainian tradition," she began when Zack set the cups on the bar. "It's called a family meeting. Are you up for it?"

"Yeah." Zack inclined his head toward his brother. "I guess I can handle it. What about you?"

"I'm here," Nick muttered.

"Hey." A man, obviously well on his way to being drunk, leaned heavily on the bar a few stools away. "Am I going to get another bourbon over here?"

"Nope." Carrying the pot, Zack crossed over. "But you can have coffee on the house."

The man scowled through red-rimmed eyes. "What the hell are you, a social worker?"

"That's me."

"I said I want a damn drink."

"You're not going to get another one here."

The drunk reached out and grabbed a handful of Zack's sweater. Considering Zack's size, Rachel took this to be a testament to the bourbon already in his system.

"This a bar or a church?"

Something flickered in Zack's eyes. Rachel recognized it, and was slipping out of her seat when Nick clamped a warning hand on hers.

"He'll handle it," he said simply.

Zack lowered his gaze to the hands on his sweater, then shifted it back to the irate customer's face. When he spoke, his voice was surprisingly mild. "Funny you should ask. I knew this guy once, down in New Orleans. He favored bourbon, too. One night he went from bar to bar, knocking them back, then staggering back out on the street. Story goes that he got so blind drunk he wandered into a church, thinking it was another bar. Weaved his way up to the front—you know,

where the altar is? Slammed his fist down and ordered himself a double. Then he dropped dead. Stone
dead." Zack pried the fingers from his sweater. "The
way I figure it, if you drink enough bourbon so you
don't know where you are, you could wake up dead in
church."

The man swore and snatched up the coffee. "I know
where the hell I am."

"That's good news. We hate hauling out corpses."

Rachel heard Nick's muffled chuckle and grinned.
"Truth or lie?" she whispered.

"Probably some of both. He always knows how to
handle the drunks."

"He wasn't doing very well with the blonde earlier."

"What blonde?"

"Another story," Rachel said, and smiled into her
coffee. "Another time. Listen, would you be more
comfortable doing this upstairs, or—" She broke off
when she heard a crash from the kitchen. "Lord, it
sounds like Rio knocked over the refrigerator." She
started to rise and go check. Then froze. The kitchen
door swung open. Rio staggered out, blood running
down his face from a wound on his forehead. Behind
him was a man in a stocking mask. He was holding a
very large gun to Rio's throat.

"Party time," he snarled, then shoved the big man
forward with the butt of the gun.

"Jumped me," Rio said in disgust as he staggered
against the bar. "Come in front upstairs."

There was a quick giggle as two more armed men,
their features distorted by their nylon masks, stepped
in. "Don't anybody move." One of them accentuated

the order by blasting away at the ship's bell over the bar. It clanged wildly.

"Lock the front door, you jerk." The first man gestured furiously. "And no shooting unless I say so. Everybody empty their pockets on the bar. Make it fast." He gestured the third man into position so that the whole bar was covered. "Wallets, jewelry, too. Hey, you." He lifted the barrel of the gun toward Lola. "Dump out those tips, sweetheart. You look like you'd earn plenty."

Nick didn't move. Couldn't. He knew the voice. Despite the distorted features, all three gunmen were easy for him to recognize. T.J.'s giggle and shambling walk. Cash's battered denim jacket. The scar on Reece's wrist where an Hombre blade had caught him.

These were his friends. His family.

"What the hell are you doing?" he demanded as T.J. pranced around the bar, scooping the take into a laundry bag.

"Empty them," Reece demanded.

"You've got to be crazy."

"Do it!" He swung the barrel toward Rachel. "And shut the hell up."

Nick kept his eyes on Reece as he complied. "This is the end, man. You crossed the line."

Behind the mask, Reece only grinned. "On the floor!" he shouted. "Facedown, hands behind your heads. Not you," he said to Zack. "You empty out the cash register. And you—" he grabbed Rachel's arm "—you look like mighty fine insurance. Anybody gets any ideas, I cash her in."

"Leave her the hell—"

"Nick!" Zack's quick and quiet order cut him off. "Back off." As he emptied the till, he watched Reece. "You don't need her."

"But I like her."

Rachel swallowed as the hand tightened on her arm, squeezing experimentally.

"Fresh meat," he called out, smacking his lips. T.J. erupted into giggles. "Maybe we'll take you along with us, sweet thing. Show you a real good time."

The furious retort burned the tip of her tongue. Rachel gritted her teeth against it. The heel of her foot on his instep, she thought. An elbow to his windpipe. She could do it, and the idea of taking him out had her blood pumping fast. But if she did, she knew the other two would open fire.

When Nick strained forward, Reece locked his arm around Rachel's throat. "Try it, dishwasher." His teeth flashed in a brutal challenge. "Do it, man. Take me on."

"Cool it." Reece's attitude toward the woman was making Cash nervous. "Come on, we came for the money. Just the money."

"I take what I want." He watched as T.J. scooped the contents of the till into his sack. "Where's the rest?"

"Slow night," Zack told him.

"Don't push me, man. There's a safe in the office. Open it."

"Fine." Zack moved slowly, passing through the opening of the bar. He had to control the urge to fight, to grab the little sneering-voiced punk and pound his face to pulp. "I'll open it as soon as you let her go."

"I got the gun," Reece reminded him. "I give the orders."

"You've got the gun," Zack agreed. "I've got the combination. You want what's in the safe, you let her go."

"Go on," Cash urged. His hands were sweating on the gun he held. "We don't need the babe. Shake her loose."

Reece felt his power slipping as Zack continued to watch him with cold blue eyes. He wanted to make them tremble. All of them. He wanted them to cry and beg. He was the head of the Cobras. He was in charge. Nobody was going to tell him any different.

"Open it," he said between his teeth. "Or I'll blow a hole in you."

"You won't get what's inside that way." Out of the corner of his eye, Zack saw Rio shift from his prone position. The big man was braced for whatever came. "This is my place," Zack continued. "I don't want anyone hurt in my place. You let the lady go, and you can take what you want."

"Let's trash the dump," T.J. shouted, and swung his gun at the glasses hanging over the bar. Shards went flying, amusing him enough to have him breaking more. "Let's kick butt and trash it." He grabbed up a vodka on the rocks and slurped it down. Then, howling, he hurled the glass to the floor.

The sound of the wreckage, and the muffled cries of the hostages on the floor, pumped Reece full of adrenaline. "Yeah, we'll trash this dump good." Over Cash's halfhearted objections, he fired at the overhead television, blasting out the screen. "That's what I'm going to do to the safe. I don't need a damn woman." He shoved Rachel aside, and she overbalanced, landing on her hands and knees. "And I don't need you."

He swung the gun toward Zack, savoring the moment. He was about to take a life, and that was new. And darkly exciting.

"This is how I give orders."

Even as Zack braced to jump, Nick was springing to his feet. Like a sprinter off the mark, he lunged, hurling full force into Zack as Reece's gun exploded.

There were screams, dozens of them. Rachel swung out with a chair, unaware that one of them was her own. She felt the chair connect, heard a grunt of pain. She caught a glimpse of the mountain that was Rio whiz past. But she was already scrambling over to where Zack and Nick lay limp on the floor.

She saw the blood. Smelled it. Her hands were smeared with it.

The room was like a madhouse around her. Shouts, crashes, running feet. She heard someone weeping. Someone else being sick.

"Oh, God. Oh, please." She was pressing her hands against Nick's chest as Zack sat up, shaking his head clear.

"Rachel. You're—" Then he saw his brother, sprawled on the floor, his face ghostly pale. And the blood seeping rapidly through his shirt. "*No!* Nick, no!" Panicked, Zack grabbed for him, fighting Rachel off as she tried to press her hands to the wound.

"Stop! You have to stop! Listen to me—keep your hands there. Keep the pressure on. I'll get a towel." With prayers whirling in her head, she scrambled up to her feet and dashed behind the bar. "Call an ambulance," she shouted. "Tell them to hurry." Because terror left no room for fumbling, she clamped down on it. Kneeling by Zack, she pushed his hands aside and pressed the folded towel on Nick's wound.

"He's young. He's strong." The tears were falling even as she felt frantically for Nick's pulse. "We're not going to let him go."

"Zack." Rio crouched down. "They got away from me. I'm sorry. I'll go after them."

"No." Revenge glittered in his eyes. "I'll go after them. Later. Get me a blanket for him, Rio. And more towels."

"I've got some." Lola passed them to Rachel, then dropped a hand on Zack's head. "He's a hero, Zack. We don't let our heroes die."

"He got in the way," Zack said as grief welled into his throat. "Damn kid was always getting in the way." He looked at Rachel, then covered her hands with his over his brother's chest. "I can't lose him."

"You won't." She heard the first wail of sirens and shuddered with relief. "We won't."

Endless hours in the waiting room, pacing, smoking, drinking bitter coffee. Zack could still see how pale Nick had been when they rushed him through Emergency and into an elevator that snapped shut in Zack's face.

Helpless. Hospitals always made him feel so helpless. Only a year had passed since he'd watched his father die in one. Slowly, inevitably, pitifully.

But not Nick. He could cling to that. Nick was young, and death wasn't inevitable when you were young.

But the blood. There had been so much blood.

He looked down at the hands that he'd scrubbed clean, and could still see his brother's life splattered across them. In his hands. That was all he could think. Nick's life had been in his hands.

"Zack." He stiffened when Rachel came up behind him and rubbed his shoulders. "How about a walk? Some fresh air?"

He just shook his head. She didn't press. It was useless to suggest he try to rest. She couldn't. Her eyes were burning, but she knew that if she closed them she would see that last horrible instant. The gun swinging toward Zack. Nick leaping. The explosion. The blood.

"I'm going to find food." Rio pushed himself off the sagging sofa. The white bandage gleamed against his dark brow. "And you're going to eat what I bring you. That boy's going to need tending soon. You can't tend when you're sick." With his lips pressed tightly together, he marched out into the hallway.

"He's crazy about Nick," Zack said, half to himself. "It's eating at him that he didn't round up three armed men all by himself."

"We'll find them, Zack."

"I thought he would hurt you. I saw it in his eyes. That kind of sickness can't be disguised by a mask. He was going to hurt somebody, wanted to hurt somebody, and he had you. I never even thought about Nick."

"It's not your fault. No," she said sharply when he tried to pull away. "I won't let you do that to yourself. There were a lot of people in that bar, and you were doing your best to protect all of them. What happened to Nick happened because he was trying to protect you. You're not going to turn an act of love into blame."

This time, when she put her arms around him, he went into them. "I need to talk to him. I don't think I could handle it if I don't get to talk to him."

"You're going to have plenty of time to talk."

"I'm sorry." Alex hesitated at the doorway. His heart was thumping, as it had been ever since he'd gotten the news. "Rachel, are you all right?"

"I'm fine." She kept one arm firm around Zack's waist as she turned. "It's Nick..."

"I know. When the call came in, I asked to handle it. I thought it would be easier on everybody." His eyes shifted to Zack's, held. "Is that okay with you?"

"Yeah. I appreciate it. I've already talked to a couple of cops."

"Why don't we sit down?" He waited while Zack sat on the edge of a chair and lit another cigarette. "Any news on your brother's condition?"

"They took him into surgery. They haven't told us anything."

"I might be able to find something out. Why don't you tell me about these three creeps?"

"They wore stocking masks," Zack began wearily. "Black clothes. One of them wore a denim jacket."

Rachel reached for Zack's hand. "The one who shot Nick was about five-eight or nine," she added. "Black hair, brown eyes. There was a scar on his left wrist. On the side, about two inches long. He wore engineer's boots, worn down at the heel."

"Good girl." Not for the first time, Alex thought that his sister would have made a damn good cop. "How about the other two?"

"The one who wanted to trash the place had a high-pitched giggle," Zack remembered. "Edgy. Skinny guy."

"About five-ten," Rachel put in. "Maybe a hundred and thirty. I didn't get a good look at him, but he had light hair. Sandy blond, I think. The third one was about the same height, but stockier. At a guess, I'd say the guns made him nervous. He was sweating a lot."

"How about age?"

"Hard to say." She looked at Zack. "Young. Early twenties?"

"About. What are the chances of catching them?"

"Better with this." Alex closed his notebook. "Look, I won't con you. It won't be easy. Now if they left prints, and the prints are on file, that's one thing. But we're going to work on it. *I'm* going to work on it," he added. "You could say I've got a vested interest."

"Yeah." Zack looked at Rachel. "I guess you do."

"Not just for her," Alex said. "I've got a stake in the kid, too. I like to see the system work, Muldoon."

"Mr. Muldoon?" A woman of about fifty dressed in green scrubs came into the room. When Zack started to rise, she gestured to him to stay where he was. "I'm Dr. Markowitz, your brother's surgeon."

"How—" He had to pause and try again. "How is he?"

"Tough." As a concession to aching feet and lower back pain, she sat on the arm of a chair. "You want all the technical jargon so I can show off, or you want the bottom line?"

The next lick of fear had his palms damp. "Bottom line."

"He's critical. And he's damn lucky, not only to have had me, but to have taken a bullet at close range that missed the heart. I put his chances now at about seventy-five percent. With luck, and the constitution of youth, we'll be able to bump that up within twenty-four hours."

The coffee churned violently in his stomach. "Are you telling me he's going to make it?"

"I'm telling you I don't like to work that hard and long on anyone and lose them. We're going to keep him in ICU for now."

"Can I see him?"

"I'll have someone come down and let you know when he's out of Recovery." She stifled a yawn and noted that she'd spent yet another sunrise in an operating room. "You want all the crap about how he'll be out for several more hours, won't know you're there, and how you should go home and get some rest?"

"No thanks."

She rubbed her eyes and smiled. "I didn't think so. He's a good-looking boy, Mr. Muldoon. I'm looking forward to chatting with him."

"Thanks. Thanks a lot."

"I'll be checking in on him." She rose, stretched, and narrowed her eyes at Alex. "Cop."

"Yes, ma'am."

"I can spot them a mile away," she said, and walked out.

Chapter Twelve

The pain was a thin sheet of agony layered under dizziness. Every time Nick surfaced, he felt it, wondered at it, then slipped away again into a cocoon of comforting unconsciousness. Sometimes he tried to speak, but the words were disjointed and senseless even to him.

He heard a disconcerting beeping, annoying and consistent, that he didn't recognize as his heartbeat on the monitor. The squeak of crepe-soled shoes against tile was muffled by the nice, steady humming in his ears. The occasional prodding and poking as his vital signs were checked and rechecked was only a minor disturbance in the huge, dark lack of awareness that covered him.

Sometimes there was a pressure on his hand, as if someone were holding it. And a murmuring—someone speaking to him. But he couldn't quite drum up the energy to listen.

Once he dreamed of the sea in a hurricane, and watched himself leap off the deck of a pitching ship into blackness.. But he never hit bottom. He just floated away.

There were other dreams. Zack standing behind him at a pinball machine, guiding his hands, laughing at the whirl of bells and whistles.

Then Cash was there, leaning on the machine, the smoke from his crooked cigarette curling up in front of his face.

He saw Rachel, smiling at him in a brightly lit room, the smell of pizza and garlic everywhere. And her eyes were bright, interested. Beautiful.

Then they were drenched with tears. Overflowing with apologies.

The old man, shouting at him. He looked so sick as he stumbled to the top of the stairs. *You'll never amount to anything. Knew it the first time I laid eyes on you.* Then that blank, slack look would come over his face, and he could only whine, *Where have you been? Where's Zack? Is he coming back soon?*

But Zack was gone, hundreds of miles away. There was no one to help.

Rio, frying potatoes and cackling over one of his own jokes. And Zack, always back to Zack, coming through the kitchen. *You going to eat all the profits, kid?* An easy grin, a friendly swipe as he went out again.

The gleaming piano—that polished dream—and Zack standing beside it, grinning foolishly. Then the glitter of the overhead light on the barrel of a gun. And Zack—

With a grunt, he threw off sleep, tried to struggle up.

"Hey, hey...take it easy, kid." Zack sprang up from the chair beside the bed to press a gentle hand on Nick's shoulder. "It's okay. You got no place to go."

He tried to focus, but the images around him kept slipping in and out like phantoms in shadows. "What?" His throat was sand-dry and aching. "Am I sick?"

"You've been better." And so have I, Zack thought, fighting to keep his hand from shaking as he lifted the plastic drinking cup. "They said you could suck on this if you came around again."

Nick took a pull of water through the straw, then another, but didn't have the energy for a third. At least his vision had cleared. He took a long, hard look at Zack. Dark circles under tired eyes in a pale face prickled by a night's growth of beard.

"You look like hell."

Grinning, Zack rubbed a hand over the stubble. "You don't look so hot yourself. Let me call a nurse."

"Nurse." Nick shook his head, almost imperceptibly, then frowned at the IV. "Is this a hospital?"

"It ain't the Ritz. You hurting?"

Nick thought about it and shook his head. "Can't tell. Feel . . . dopey."

"Well, you are." Swamped with relief, Zack laid a hand on Nick's cheek, left it there until embarrassment had it dropping away. "You're such a jerk, Nick."

Nick was too bleary to hear the catch in Zack's voice. "Was there an accident? I..." And then it came flooding back, a tidal wave of memory. "At the bar." His hand fisted on the sheets. "Rachel? Is Rachel all right?"

"She's fine. Been in and out of here. I had Rio browbeat her into getting something to eat."

"You." Nick took another long look to reassure himself. "He didn't shoot you."

"No, you idiot." His voice broke, then roughened. "He shot *you*."

When his legs went watery, Zack sat again, buried his face in his hands. The hands were trembling. Nick stared, utterly amazed, as this man he'd always thought was the next best thing to superhuman struggled for composure.

"I could kill you for scaring me like this. If you weren't flat on your back already, I'd damn well put you there."

But insults and threats delivered in a shaky voice held little power. "Hey." Nick lifted a hand, but wasn't sure what to do with it. "You okay?"

"No, I'm not okay," Zack tossed back, and rose to pace to the window. He stared out, seeing nothing, until he felt some portion of control again. "Yeah, yeah, I'm fine. Looks like you're going to be that way, too. They said they'd move you down to a regular room sometime soon, if you rated it."

"Where am I now?" Curious, Nick turned his head to study the room. Glass walls and blinking, beeping machines. "Wow, high tech. How long have I been out?"

"You came around a couple times before. They said you wouldn't remember. You babbled a lot."

"Oh, yeah. About what?"

"Pinball machines." Steadier now, Zack walked back to the bed. "Some girl named Marcie or Marlie. Remind me to pump you on that little number later."

It pleased him to see a faint smile curve Nick's lips. "You asked for french fries."

"What can I say? It's a weakness. Did I get any?"

"No. Maybe we'll sneak some in later. Are you hungry?"

"I don't know. You didn't tell me how long."

Zack reached for a cigarette, remembered, and sighed. "About twelve hours since they finished cutting you up and sewing you back together. I figure if he'd shot you in the head instead of the chest, you'd have walked away whistling." He tapped his knuckles on Nick's temple. "Hard as a rock. I owe you one, a big one."

"No, you don't."

"You saved my life."

Nick let his heavy lids close. "It's kind of like jumping off a ship in a hurricane. You don't think about it. Know what I mean?"

"Yeah."

"Zack?"

"Right here."

"I want to talk to a cop."

"You've got to rest."

"I need to talk to a cop," Nick said again as he drifted off. "I know who they were."

Zack watched him sleep and, since there was no one to see, brushed gently at the hair on his brother's forehead.

"I told you his condition is good," Dr. Markowitz repeated. "Go home, Mr. Muldoon."

"Not a chance." Zack leaned against the wall beside the door to Nick's room. He was feeling a great deal better since they'd brought his brother out of ICU, but he wasn't ready to jump ship.

"God save me from stubborn Irishmen." She aimed a hard look at Rachel. "Mrs. Muldoon, do you have any influence with him?"

"I'm not Mrs. Muldoon, and no. I think we might pry him away once he checks in on Nick. My brother shouldn't be with him much longer."

"Your brother's the cop?" She sighed and shook her head. "All right. I'll give you five minutes with my patient, then you're out of here. Believe me, I'll call Security and have them toss you out if necessary."

"Yes, ma'am."

"That goes for that giant who's been lurking around the corridors, too."

"I'll take them both home," Rachel promised. She looked around quickly as the door opened. "Alexi?"

"We're finished." He couldn't keep the satisfied gleam out of his eyes. "I've got some rounding up to do."

"He identified them?" Zack demanded.

"Cold. And he's raring to testify."

"I want—"

"No chance," Alex said quickly, noting Zack's clenched fists. "The kid figured out how to do it the right way, Muldoon. Take a lesson. Keep him in line, Rach."

"I'll try," she murmured as her brother hurried off. "Zack, if you're going in there to talk to him, pull it together."

"That son of a bitch shot my brother."

"And he'll pay for it."

With a curt nod, Zack walked by her and into Nick's room. He stood at the foot of the bed, waiting. "How are you feeling?"

"Okay." He was exhausted after his interview with Alex, but he wasn't finished. "I need to talk to you, to tell you. Explain."

"It can wait."

"No. It was my fault. The whole thing. They were Cobras, Zack. They knew when to come in and how, because I told them. I didn't know... I swear to God I didn't know what they were going to do. I don't expect you to believe me."

Zack waited a moment until he got his bearings. "Why shouldn't I believe you?"

Nick squeezed his eyes tight. "I messed up. Like always." He poured out the entire story of how he'd run into Cash at the arcade. "I thought we were just talking. And all the time he was setting me up. Setting you up."

"You trusted him." Zack came around the side of the bed to put a hand on Nick's wrist. "You thought he was your friend. That's not messing up, Nick, it's just trusting people who don't deserve it. You're not like them." When Nick's eyes opened again, Zack took a firm hold of his hand. "If you messed up anything, it was yourself by trying to be like them. And that's done."

"I won't let them get away with it."

"*We* won't," Zack told him. "We're in this together."

"Yeah," Nick said on a long breath. "Okay."

"They're going to kick me out of here so you can get some rest. I'll be back tomorrow."

"Zack," Nick called out as his brother hit the door. "Don't forget the fries."

"You got it."

"Okay?" Rachel asked when Zack came out.

"Okay." Then he gathered her up, held her hard and close. She was slim and small, and as steady as an anchor in a storm-tossed sea. "Come home with me, please," he murmured against her hair. "Stay with me tonight."

"Let's go." She pressed a kiss to his cheek. "I can buy a toothbrush on the way."

Later, when he fell into an exhausted sleep, she lay beside him and kept watch. She knew it was the first time he'd done more than nod off in a chair in nearly forty-eight hours. Odd, she thought as she watched his face in the faint, shadowy light that sneaked through the windows. She'd never considered herself the nurturing type. But it had been very satisfying to simply lie beside him and hold him until the strain and fatigue of the past few days had toppled him into sleep.

The bigger they are, she thought again, pressing a light kiss to his forehead.

Still, as tired as she was, and as relieved, she couldn't find escape in sleep herself. How daunting it was to realize she'd come to a point in her life where she wasn't sure of her moves.

Love didn't run on logic. It didn't follow neat lines or a list of priorities. Yet, in a matter of days, the bond that had brought them together would be broken. They would go into court, and it would be resolved one way or the other.

Now was the time to face the what-happens-next.

He'd asked her to move in with him. Rachel shifted to watch the pattern of shadows on the ceiling. It could be enough. Or much too much. Her problem now was to decide what she could live with, and what she could live without.

She was very much afraid that the one thing she couldn't live without was sleeping beside her.

He shuddered once, made a strangled sound in his throat before ripping himself awake. Instantly she moved to soothe.

"Shh..." She touched a hand to his cheek, to his shoulder, stroking. "It's all right. Everything's all right."

"Hurricanes," he murmured, groggy. "I'll tell you about it sometime."

"Okay." She rested a hand on his heart, as if to slow its rapid pace. "Go back to sleep, Muldoon. You're worn out."

"It's nice that you're here. Real nice."

"I like it, too." One brow arched as she felt his hand slide up her thigh. "Don't start something you won't be able to finish."

"I just want my T-shirt back." He moved his hand up her makeshift nightie until her warm, soft breast filled his palm. Comfort. Arousal. Perfection. "Just as I thought. This is a completely nonregulation body."

The stirring started low and deep, working its way through her. "You're pushing your luck."

"I was having this dream about the navy." His fatigue had everything moving in slow motion, making it all the more erotic when he slipped the shirt up and off. Her arms seemed to flow over her head and down again like water. "It makes me remember what it was

like being at sea for months without seeing a woman."
He lowered his mouth to flick his tongue over her. "Or
tasting one."

She sighed luxuriously, and even that slight move-
ment heightened his need. "Tell me more." His mouth
met hers, so soft, so sweet.

"When I woke up just now, I could smell your hair,
your skin. I've been waking up wanting you for weeks.
Now I can wake up and have you."

"Just that easy, huh?"

"Yeah." He lifted his head and smiled down at her.
"Just that easy."

She trailed a finger down his back as she considered. "I've got only one thing to say to you, Muldoon."

"What?"

"All hands on deck." With a laugh, she rolled on
top of him.

And it was very, very easy.

"You're not being sensible," she said to Nick as she
walked up the courthouse steps beside him, support-
ing his arm. "It's the simplest thing in the world to get
a postponement under the circumstances."

"I want it over," he repeated, and glanced over at
Zack.

"I'm with you."

"Far be it from me to fight the pair of you," she
said in disgust. "If you keel over—"

"I'm not an invalid."

"You're two days out of the hospital," she pointed
out.

"Dr. Markowitz gave him the green light," Zack
put in.

"I don't care what Dr. Markowitz gave him."

"Rachel." A little winded from the climb, but still game, Nick shook off her hand. "Stop playing mother."

"Fine." She tossed up her hands, then lowered them again to fuss with Nick's tie, brush the shoulders of his jacket. She caught Zack's grin over Nick's shoulder and scowled. "Shut up, Muldoon."

"Aye, aye, sir."

"He thinks he's so cute with the nautical talk." She stood back to study her client. He was still a little pale, but he would do. "Now, are you sure you remember everything I explained to you?"

"Rachel, you went over the drill a dozen times." Letting out a huff of breath, he turned to his brother. "Can I have a minute with her?"

"Sure." Zack tossed a look over his shoulder. "Hands off."

"Yeah, yeah." The smirk was back, but it was good-natured rather than nasty. "Listen, Rachel, first I want to tell you how... Well, it was really nice of your family to come by the hospital the way they did. Your mom—" he pushed restless hands in his pockets, then pulled them out again "—bringing me cookies, and all the other stuff. Your father, coming by to hang out and play checkers."

It should have sounded corny, he reflected. But it didn't.

"They came to see you because they wanted to."

"Yeah, but... well, it was nice. I even got a card from Freddie. And the cop—he was okay."

"Alex has his moments."

"What I'm trying to say is, whatever happens today, you've done a lot for me. Maybe I don't know where I'm going, but I know where I'm not. I owe that to you."

"No, you don't." Worried she might cry, she made her tone brisk. "A little, sure, but most of it was right here." She tapped a finger on his heart. "You're okay, LeBeck."

"Thanks. One more thing." He glanced over to be sure Zack was out of earshot. "I know I made things a little sticky before. Zack's been making noises that you might be moving in. I just wanted you to know that I wouldn't be in the way."

"I haven't decided what I'm going to do. Regardless, you wouldn't be in the way. You're family. Got it?"

His lips curved. "I'm getting it. If you decide to throw him over, I'm available."

"I'll keep it in mind." She gave his jacket one last tug. "Let's go."

There was no reason to be nervous, she told herself as she led Nick to the defense table. Her statement was well prepared, and she had a sympathetic judge on the bench.

She was terrified.

She rose with the rest of the court when Judge Beckett came in. Ignoring the twisting in her gut, she gave Nick a quick, confident smile.

"Well, well, Mr. LeBeck," Beckett began, folding her hands. "How time flies. I hear through the grapevine that you ran into a bit of trouble recently. Are you quite recovered?"

"Your Honor..." Puzzled by the break in courtroom routine, Rachel rose.

"Sit, sit, sit." Beckett gestured with the back of her hand. "Mr. LeBeck, I asked how you're feeling."

"I'm okay."

"Good. I'm also informed that you identified the three desperadoes who broke into Mr. Muldoon's bar. Three members of the Cobras—an organization with which you were associated, I believe—who are now in custody awaiting trial."

Rachel tried again. "Your Honor, in my final report—"

"I read it, thank you, Counselor. You did an excellent job. I'd prefer to hear from Mr. LeBeck directly. My question is, why did you identify these men, who a relatively short time ago you chose to protect?"

"Stand up," Rachel hissed under her breath.

Frowning, Nick complied. "Ma'am?"

"Was the question unclear? Shall I repeat it?"

"No, I got it."

"Excellent. And your answer?"

"They messed with my brother."

"Ah." As if she were a teacher congratulating a much-improved student, Beckett smiled. "And that changes the complexion of things."

Forgetting all Rachel's prompting, he took the natural stance. The aggressive one. "Listen, they broke in, busted Rio's head open, shoved Rachel around and waved guns all over the place. It wasn't right. Maybe you think turning them in makes me a creep, but Reece was going to shoot my brother. No way he was going to walk from that."

"What I think it makes you, LeBeck, is a clear-thinking, potentially responsible adult who has grasped not only the basic tenets of right and wrong, but also of loyalty, which is often more valuable. You will likely make more mistakes in your life, but I doubt you will make the kind that will bring you back into my courtroom. Now, I believe the district attorney has something to say."

"Yes, Your Honor. The state drops all charges against Nicholas LeBeck."

"All *right!*" Rachel said, springing to her feet.

"Is that it?" Nick managed.

"Not quite." Beckett pulled the attention back to the bench. "I get to do this." She slapped the gavel down. "Now that's it."

With a laugh, Rachel threw her arms around Nick's neck. "You did it," she murmured to him. "I want you to remember that. You did it."

"I'm not going to jail." He hadn't been able to allow anyone, even himself, to see how much that had terrified him. He gave Rachel one last squeeze before turning to Zack. "I'm going home."

"That's right." Zack held out a hand. Then, with an oath, he dragged Nick into a hug. "Play your cards right, kid, I'll even give you a raise."

"Raise, my butt. I'm working my way up to partner."

"If you gentlemen will excuse me, I have other clients." She gave each of them a highly unprofessional kiss.

"We have to celebrate." Zack caught her hands. There was nothing he could say. Too much that needed to be said. "Seven o'clock, at the bar. Be there."

"I wouldn't miss it."

"Rachel," Nick called out, "you're the best."

"No." She tossed a laugh over her shoulder. "But I will be."

* * *

She was a little late. It couldn't be helped. How could she have known she'd get a case of criminal assault tossed at her at six o'clock?

Two years with the PD's office, she reminded herself, grinning a little, as she pushed open the door of the bar.

When the cheer went up, she stopped cold. There were streamers, balloons, and several people in incredibly stupid party hats. A huge banner hung across the back wall.

Next to Rachel, Perry Mason is a Wimp.

It made her laugh, even as Rio hauled her onto his shoulders and carried her to the bar. He set her down, and someone thrust a glass of champagne in her hand.

"Some party."

Zack tugged at her hair until she turned her face for a kiss. "I tried to make them wait for you, but they got caught up."

"*I'll* catch up..." she began. Then her mouth dropped open. "Mama?"

"We've already eating Rio's short ribs," Nadia informed her. "Now your papa is going to dance with me."

"Maybe I dance with you later," Yuri informed his daughter as he swept Nadia off for what was surely to be a polka.

"You invited my parents. And—" She shook her head in wonder. "That's Alex stuffing meatballs in his face."

"It's a private party." Zack clinked his glass against hers. "Nick made up the list. Take a look."

She craned her neck and spotted him at a table. "Isn't that Lola's daughter?"

"She's really impressed that he's been shot."

"It's one of the top ten ways to impress a woman."

"I'll keep it in mind. Want to dance?"

She took another sip of champagne. "I'd bet a week's pay you don't know how to polka."

"You lose," he said, and grabbed her hand.

It went on for hours. Rachel lost track of the time as she sampled the enormous spread Rio had prepared and washed it down with champagne. She danced until her feet went numb and ultimately collapsed to sing Ukrainian folk songs with her slightly snookered father.

"Good party," Yuri said, swaying a bit, while his wife helped him into his coat.

"Yes, Papa."

He grinned as he leaned toward Rachel. "Now I go home and make your mama feel like a girl."

"Big talk. You'll snore in truck on the way home."

He leered at his wife. "Then you wake me up."

"Maybe." She kissed her daughter. "You make me very proud."

"Thank you, Mama."

"You're a smart girl, Rachel. I'll tell you what you should already know. When you find a good man, you lose nothing by taking hold, and everything by letting go. You understand me?"

"Yes, Mama." Rachel looked over at Zack. "I think I do."

"This is good."

Rachel watched them walk out, arm in arm.

"They're pretty great," Nick said from behind her.

"Yes, they are."

"And your brother's not so bad—for a cop."

"I'm pretty fond of him, all in all." With a sigh, she brushed a streamer from her hair. "Looks like the party's over."

"This one is." Smiling to himself, he turned away to help Rio gather up some of the mess. If Nick knew his brother—and he was beginning to believe he did—Rachel was in for another surprise before the evening was over.

Zack tolerated the cleanup crew for nearly twenty minutes before ordering Rio home and Nick to bed. If he didn't get Rachel to himself, he was going to explode. "We'll get the rest tomorrow."

"You're the boss." Rio gave Rachel a wink as he shrugged into his coat. "For the time being."

Zack shook a nearly empty bottle. "There's a little champagne left. How about it?"

"I think I could choke it down." She settled at the bar and, aiming her best provocative look at him, held out her glass. "Buy me a drink, sailor?"

"Be my pleasure." After filling her glass, he slid the bottle aside. "There's nothing I can say or do to repay you."

"Don't start."

"I want you to know how much I appreciate everything. You made all the difference."

"I was doing my job, and following my conscience. No one needs to thank me for that."

"Damn it, Rachel, let me explain how I feel."

Nick swung in from the kitchen. "If that's the best you can do, bro, you need all the help you can get."

The single glance Zack shot in his direction was explosive. "Go to bed."

"On my way." But he walked to the juke and popped in a few quarters. After punching some buttons, he turned back to them. "You two are a real case. Take it from someone who knows you both have weaknesses, and cut to the chase." With a shake of his head, he dimmed the lights and walked out.

"What the hell was that?" Zack demanded.

"Don't ask me. Weaknesses? I don't have any weaknesses."

Zack grinned at her. "Me either." He came around the bar. "But it's nice music."

"Real nice," she agreed, going willingly into his arms to sway there.

"Things have been a little hectic."

"Hmm . . . Just a little."

"I'd like to talk to you about what I asked you a while back. About moving in."

She shut her eyes. She'd already decided the answer was no. As hard as it was to resist a half a loaf, she would hold out for the whole one. "This may not be the time to go into it."

"I can't think of a better one. The thing is, Rachel, I don't want you to move in."

"You—" She stiffened, then shoved away, nearly toppling him over. "Well, that's just fine."

"What I want—"

"Stuff what you want," she tossed back at him. "Isn't that just typical? After I clean up the mess for you, you brush me off."

"I'm not—"

"Shut up, Muldoon. I'll have my say."

"Who could stop you?" he muttered.

Her heels slapped the floor as she tried to walk off her anger. "You're out of order, Buster. You're the one who kept pushing your way in, pushing your way in." She demonstrated by making shoving motions with her hands. "Just wouldn't take no for an answer."

"You didn't say no," he reminded her.

"That's irrelevant." Facing him, she fisted her hands on her hips. "So, you don't want me to move in. Fine. My answer was an unqualified no anyway."

"Great." He stepped closer so that he had to lean over to shout in her face. "Because I'm not settling for you packing up a few things and coming by to play house. I want you to marry me."

"And if you think— Oh, God." She swayed back, forward, then pressed a hand to his chest for balance. "I have to sit down."

"So sit." He nipped her around the waist and plopped her down on the bar. "And just listen. I know we said no long-term commitments. You didn't want them, and neither did I. But we're turning the page here, Rachel, and there's a whole new set of rules."

"Zack, I—"

"No. You're not going to get me tangled up in an argument." She was too good at winning those, and he'd be damned if he was going to lose this time. "I've thought this through. You've got your priorities, and that's fine." He grabbed her hands, hard. Rachel decided she'd check for broken fingers later. Right now, she couldn't feel anything but amazement. "All you have to do is add one to the list. Me. I didn't plan on falling in love with you, but that's the way it is, so deal with it."

"Me either," she murmured, but he plowed on.

"Maybe you think you don't have room..." His grip tightened, and he ignored her quick yelp. "What did you say?"

"I said, 'Me either.'"

"'Me either' what?"

"You said, 'I didn't plan on falling in love with you,' and I said, 'Me either.'" She let out a long, shaky sigh when his hands slid limply from hers. "But that's the way it is, so deal with it."

"Oh, yeah?"

"Yeah." Perched on the bar, she linked her arms around his neck, lowered her brow to his. Amazing, she thought. He was as scared as she was. "You beat me to it, Muldoon. I was going to turn you down because I love you too much, and I wasn't going to settle for anything less with you than everything. It's had me going in circles for days."

"Weeks." He brought his mouth to hers. "I was going to try to ease you into it, but I couldn't wait. I even talked to your father about my intentions tonight."

Unsure whether to laugh or groan, she drew back. "You did not."

"I plied him with vodka first, just in case. He told me he wanted more grandchildren."

She felt her heart swell. "I'd like to accommodate him."

Something caught in his chest, then broke beautifully free. "No kidding?"

And here it was, she thought, looking down into his eyes. A whole new set of rules. A whole new life for the taking. "No kidding. I want a family with you. I want it all with you. That's my choice."

He cupped her face in his hands. "You're everything I've wanted and never thought I'd have."

"You're everything I wanted," she repeated. "And pretended not to." When she lowered her lips to his, she felt the sting of tears in her throat. "We're not going to get sloppy, are we, Muldoon?"

"Who, us?" He grinned as she slid off the bar and into his arms. "Not a chance."

A Note from the Author

I happen to feel I'm an expert on womanhood as I've been surrounded by men all my life. I was the youngest of five and the only daughter. Outnumbered. This meant learning to use basic female traits to my advantage. Now, I'm not talking about wimpy tears and whining. Though they have their uses. I'm talking about the female mind, with all its interesting twists and angles. And the female heart, with its deep wells and often incomprehensible logic. As a girl, I learned to appreciate and to enjoy femininity, the kind that has nothing to do with lace and flounces and everything to do with emotion.

It was fortunate I learned—I now have a husband and two sons and am once more outnumbered.

When I first met Rachel Stanislaski, she was a law student, the youngest child and second daughter of Ukrainian immigrants. Though I found each and every member of the Stanislaski family fascinating, Rachel was special because of her personal ambitions, the strength of her convictions and the way they merged and melded with her strong love of family.

When I met Zack Muldoon, I knew it would take a very special woman to match him. Rachel, with her wit, her temper, her sense of justice and her deep well of compassion, fit the bill.

I'm delighted to participate in Silhouette's celebration of womanhood, and hope that Rachel will hold a special place in your heart. She does in mine.

*   *   *   *   *

Take 4 bestselling love stories FREE

Plus get a FREE surprise gift!

Silhouette

SPECIAL EDITION™

That SPECIAL Woman!

She's friend, wife, mother—she's you!
And to thank you for being so special to us,
we would like to send you a

FREE

Romantic Journal

in which to record all of *your*
special moments.

To receive your free ROMANTIC JOURNAL, send four proof-of-purchase coupons from any Silhouette Special Edition THAT SPECIAL WOMAN! title from January to June, plus $3.00 for postage and handling (check or money order—please do not send cash) payable to Silhouette Books, to: **In the U.S.:** THAT SPECIAL WOMAN!, Silhouette Books, 3010 Walden Avenue, P.O. Box 1396, Buffalo, NY 14269-1396; **In Canada:** THAT SPECIAL WOMAN!, Silhouette Books, P.O. Box 609, Fort Erie, Ontario L2A 5X3.

087 KAS

NAME: _____

ADDRESS: _____

CITY: _____ STATE/PROV: _____ ZIP/POSTAL: _____

(Please allow 4-6 weeks for delivery. Hurry! Quantities are limited. Offer expires August 31, 1993.)

That SPECIAL Woman!

Proof of Purchase

087 KAS